AZURICA

Power Crystal

Once a Star Darling has granted her first wish
and returns to Starland, she receives a very
special treasure—a beautiful Power Crystal.

WATCH

Wish Pendant

A Wish Pendant is a powerful accessory worn
by a Star Darling. On Wishworld, it helps
her identify her Wisher and stores the
ever-important wish energy.

To an amazing reader:

Jalisa Gettings

Adora Finds a Friend

Adora Finds a Friend

Shana Muldoon Zappa and Ahmet Zappa
with Zelda Rose

Disney Press

Los Angeles • New York

Copyright © 2016 Disney Enterprises, Inc.

All rights reserved. Published by Disney Press, an imprint of Disney
Book Group. No part of this book may be reproduced or transmitted
in any form or by any means, electronic or mechanical, including
photocopying, recording, or by any information storage and retrieval
system, without written permission from the publisher.
For information address Disney Press,
1101 Flower Street, Glendale, California 91201.

Printed in the United States of America
Reinforced Binding
First Paperback Edition, June 2016
1 3 5 7 9 10 8 6 4 2

FAC-025438-16113

Library of Congress Control Number: 2016930814
ISBN 978-1-4847-1429-4

For more Disney Press fun, visit www.disneybooks.com

Halo Violetta Zappa. You are pure light, joy, and inspiration. We love you soooooo much.

May the Star Darlings continue to shine brightly upon you. May every step upon your path be blessed with positivity and the understanding that you have the power within you to manifest the most fulfilling life you can possibly dream of and more. May you always remember that being different and true to yourself makes your inner star shine brighter. And never ever stop making wishes.

Glow for it. . . .
Mommy and Daddy

And to everyone else here on "Wishworld":

May you realize that no matter where you are in life, no matter what you look like or where you were born, you, too, have the power within you to create the life of your dreams. Through celebrating your own uniqueness, thinking positively, and taking action, you can make your wishes come true. May you understand that you are never alone. There is always someone near who will understand you if you look hard enough. The Star Darlings are here to remind you that there is an unstoppable energy to staying positive, wishing, and believing in yourself. That inner star shines within you.

Smile. The Star Darlings have your back. We know how startastic you truly are.

Glow for it. . . .
Your friends,
Shana and Ahmet

Student Reports

NAME: Clover
BRIGHT DAY: January 5
FAVORITE COLOR: Purple
INTERESTS: Music, painting, studying
WISH: To be the best songwriter and DJ on Starland
WHY CHOSEN: Clover has great self-discipline, patience, and willpower. She is creative, responsible, dependable, and extremely loyal.
WATCH OUT FOR: Clover can be hard to read and she is reserved with those she doesn't know. She's afraid to take risks and can be a wisecracker at times.
SCHOOL YEAR: Second
POWER CRYSTAL: Panthera
WISH PENDANT: Barrette

* • • *• • *• • *• • *

NAME: Adora
BRIGHT DAY: February 14
FAVORITE COLOR: Sky blue
INTERESTS: Science, thinking about the future and how she can make it better
WISH: To be the top fashion designer on Starland
WHY CHOSEN: Adora is clever and popular and cares about the world around her. She's a deep thinker.
WATCH OUT FOR: Adora can have her head in the clouds and be thinking about other things.
SCHOOL YEAR: Third
POWER CRYSTAL: Azurica
WISH PENDANT: Watch

* • • *• • *• • *• • *

NAME: Piper
BRIGHT DAY: March 4
FAVORITE COLOR: Seafoam green
INTERESTS: Composing poetry and writing in her dream journal
WISH: To become the best version of herself she can possibly be and to share that by writing books
WHY CHOSEN: Piper is giving, kind, and sensitive. She is very intuitive and aware.
WATCH OUT FOR: Piper can be dreamy, absentminded, and wishy-washy. She can also be moody and easily swayed by the opinions of others.
SCHOOL YEAR: Second
POWER CRYSTAL: Dreamalite
WISH PENDANT: Bracelets

Starling Academy

NAME: Astra
BRIGHT DAY: April 9
FAVORITE COLOR: Red
INTERESTS: Individual sports
WISH: To be the best athlete on Starland—to win!
WHY CHOSEN: Astra is energetic, brave, clever, and confident. She has boundless energy and is always direct and to the point.
WATCH OUT FOR: Astra is sometimes cocky, self-centered, condescending, and brash.
SCHOOL YEAR: Second
POWER CRYSTAL: Quarrelite
WISH PENDANT: Wristbands

* • • * • • ━ ◆ ━ • • * • • *

NAME: Tessa
BRIGHT DAY: May 18
FAVORITE COLOR: Emerald green
INTERESTS: Food, flowers, love
WISH: To be successful enough that she can enjoy a life of luxury
WHY CHOSEN: Tessa is warm, charming, affectionate, trustworthy, and dependable. She has incredible drive and commitment.
WATCH OUT FOR: Tessa does not like to be rushed. She can be quite stubborn and often says no. She does not deal well with change and is prone to exaggeration. She can be easily sidetracked.
SCHOOL YEAR: Third
POWER CRYSTAL: Gossamer
WISH PENDANT: Brooch

* • • * • • ━ ◆ ━ • • * • • *

NAME: Gemma
BRIGHT DAY: June 2
FAVORITE COLOR: Orange
INTERESTS: Sharing her thoughts about almost anything
WISH: To be valued for her opinions on everything
WHY CHOSEN: Gemma is friendly, easygoing, funny, extroverted, and social. She knows a little bit about everything.
WATCH OUT FOR: Gemma talks—a lot—and can be a little too honest sometimes and offend others. She can have a short attention span and can be superficial.
SCHOOL YEAR: First
POWER CRYSTAL: Scatterite
WISH PENDANT: Earrings

Student Reports

NAME: Cassie
BRIGHT DAY: July 6
FAVORITE COLOR: White
INTERESTS: Reading, crafting
WISH: To be more independent and confident and less fearful
WHY CHOSEN: Cassie is extremely imaginative and artistic. She is a voracious reader and is loyal, caring, and a good friend. She is very intuitive.
WATCH OUT FOR: Cassie can be distrustful, jealous, moody, and brooding.
SCHOOL YEAR: First
POWER CRYSTAL: Lunalite
WISH PENDANT: Glasses

****

NAME: Leona
BRIGHT DAY: August 16
FAVORITE COLOR: Gold
INTERESTS: Acting, performing, dressing up
WISH: To be the most famous pop star on Starland
WHY CHOSEN: Leona is confident, hardworking, generous, open-minded, optimistic, caring, and a strong leader.
WATCH OUT FOR: Leona can be vain, opinionated, selfish, bossy, dramatic, and stubborn and is prone to losing her temper.
SCHOOL YEAR: Third
POWER CRYSTAL: Glisten paw
WISH PENDANT: Cuff

****

NAME: Vega
BRIGHT DAY: September 1
FAVORITE COLOR: Blue
INTERESTS: Exercising, analyzing, cleaning, solving puzzles
WISH: To be the top student at Starling Academy
WHY CHOSEN: Vega is reliable, observant, organized, and very focused.
WATCH OUT FOR: Vega can be opinionated about everything, and she can be fussy, uptight, critical, arrogant, and easily embarrassed.
SCHOOL YEAR: Second
POWER CRYSTAL: Queezle
WISH PENDANT: Belt

Starling Academy

NAME: Libby
BRIGHT DAY: October 12
FAVORITE COLOR: Pink
INTERESTS: Helping others, interior design, art, dancing
WISH: To give everyone what they need—both on Starland and through wish granting on Wishworld
WHY CHOSEN: Libby is generous, articulate, gracious, diplomatic, and kind.
WATCH OUT FOR: Libby can be indecisive and may try too hard to please everyone.
SCHOOL YEAR: First
POWER CRYSTAL: Charmelite
WISH PENDANT: Necklace

* ·· * ·· * ·· * ·· * ·· *

NAME: Scarlet
BRIGHT DAY: November 3
FAVORITE COLOR: Black
INTERESTS: Crystal climbing (and other extreme sports), magic, thrill seeking
WISH: To live on Wishworld
WHY CHOSEN: Scarlet is confident, intense, passionate, magnetic, curious, and very brave.
WATCH OUT FOR: Scarlet is a loner and can alienate others by being secretive, arrogant, stubborn, and jealous.
SCHOOL YEAR: Third
POWER CRYSTAL: Ravenstone
WISH PENDANT: Boots

* ·· * ·· * ·· * ·· * ·· *

NAME: Sage
BRIGHT DAY: December 1
FAVORITE COLOR: Lavender
INTERESTS: Travel, adventure, telling stories, nature, and philosophy
WISH: To become the best Wish-Granter Starland has ever seen
WHY CHOSEN: Sage is honest, adventurous, curious, optimistic, friendly, and relaxed.
WATCH OUT FOR: Sage has a quick temper! She can also be restless, irresponsible, and too trusting of others' opinions. She may jump to conclusions.
SCHOOL YEAR: First
POWER CRYSTAL: Lavenderite
WISH PENDANT: Necklace

Introduction

You take a deep breath, about to blow out the candles on your birthday cake. Clutching a coin in your fist, you get ready to toss it into the dancing waters of a fountain. You stare at your little brother as you each hold an end of a dried wishbone, about to pull. But what do you do first?

You make a wish, of course!

Ever wonder what happens right after you make that wish? *Not much*, you may be thinking.

Well, you'd be wrong.

Because something quite unexpected happens next. Each and every wish that is made becomes a glowing Wish Orb, invisible to the human eye. This undetectable orb zips through the air and into the heavens, on a one-way trip to the brightest star in the sky—a magnificent place called Starland. Starland is inhabited by Starlings, who look a lot like you and me, except they have a sparkly glow to their skin, and glittery hair in unique colors. And they have one more thing: magical powers. The Starlings use these powers to make good wishes come true, for when good wishes are granted, the result is positive energy. And the Starlings of Starland need this energy to keep their world running.

In case you are wondering, there are three kinds of Wish Orbs:

1) GOOD WISH ORBS. These wishes are positive and helpful and come from the heart. They are pretty and sparkly and are nurtured in climate-controlled Wish-Houses. They bloom into fantastical glowing orbs. When the time is right, they are presented to the appropriate Starling for wish fulfillment.

2) BAD WISH ORBS. These are for selfish, mean-spirited, or negative things. They don't sparkle

at all. They are immediately transported to a special containment center, as they are very dangerous and must not be granted.

3) IMPOSSIBLE WISH ORBS. These wishes are for things, like world peace and disease cures, that simply can't be granted by Starlings. These sparkle with an almost impossibly bright light and are taken to a special area of the Wish-House with tinted windows to contain the glare they produce. The hope is that one day they can be turned into good wishes the Starlings can help grant.

Starlings take their wish granting very seriously. There is a special school, called Starling Academy, that accepts only the best and brightest young Starling girls. They study hard for four years, and when they graduate, they are ready to start traveling to Wishworld to help grant wishes. For as long as anyone can remember, only graduates of wish-granting schools have ever been allowed to travel to Wishworld. But things have changed in a very big way.

Read on for the rest of the story. . . .

Prologue

TO: Sage, Libby, Leona, Vega, Piper, Astra, Adora, Clover, and Gemma

FROM: Cassie

INSTRUCTIONS: Auto-delivery of this holo-letter scheduled for Reliquaday, in three starhours' time

Dear Star Darlings,

Greetings and salutations, friends and fellow Star Darlings. You may be wondering why I'm sending a holo-letter when I've just seen you all at the ceremony. (Starkudos, Tessa, on a successful mission!) There are many answers to that question. And I'll get to the most important one at the end of this holo-letter. So keep reading.

In short, I am writing to clarify the dangerous situation on Starland and, in doing so, explain my own actions. Wait! Don't delete this letter! Please hear me out! (This means you, Sage and Libby, who have turned a blind eye to Lady Stella's involvement.) And don't roll your eyes. (This means you, Adora! I do not overreact to problems.) I am not imagining that Starland is in major trouble. It is. I am not imagining conspiracies or villains. They exist.

To support my stand, here are the issues in no particular order:

The Issues on Wishworld: Problematic Missions

Why do the Star Darlings even exist? As we all know, Lady Stella brought us together to test her theory that if the wishes of young Wishlings were to be granted by young Starlings, this special combination would produce an even greater amount of positive wish energy than older Starlings could ever collect. And now, since we know that Starland

is having a serious wish energy crisis, our wish
missions are even more important than ever.

*Why are our Wish Missions—even the successful
ones—always in danger until the last starmin?* We've
been trained and schooled and are starmendously
capable, yet something always goes wrong. And that
does not even take Leona's mission into account.
Not only was her Wish Pendant destroyed, making
it impossible for it to absorb any wish energy, but
she almost didn't make it back on her shooting star!
And she obviously (sorry, Leona!) didn't get her
Power Crystal.

The Issues with Star Darlings: 1) Fighting within
Our Group and 2) Strange Behavior
(Both designed to keep us from acting together and
from acting at all!)

Specifically:

Why were we fighting with our roommates? The
poisonous flowers from the Isle of Misera that
were placed in our rooms.

*Why were all the Star Kindness Day compliments
changed to insults?* That one speaks for itself!

Why were we all acting so odd and not even realizing it?
Because of the poisonous nail polish from the Star
Darlings–only mani-pedi party! Whoever created
the polish knew this strange behavior would
interfere with our missions. Not to mention it was
starmendously embarrassing for everyone (Libby's
falling asleep anywhere and everywhere; Scarlet's
skipping anywhere and everywhere; and probably
the worst: my bragging anywhere and everywhere).

Additional Star Darlings Issues: the Band and the Star-Zap

*Why was Leona's band named the Star Darlings, with
tryout info sent to the whole school?* To bring our secret
group into the starlight is my guess!

Why was my Star-Zap not working properly?
So someone could intercept Star Darlings
communication. Again, that's my guess.

My Issue with Lady Stella: She Is Responsible for All This

(Again, Sage and Libby: hear me out.)

Specifically:

Why was Scarlet kicked out of the Star Darlings and replaced with Ophelia? To sabotage a mission, of course.

And who set that in motion? Lady Stella! She switched admissions test results so it looked like Scarlet had low scores and Ophelia's were high as the moons. (Starkudos to Scarlet. Impressive work, really!) Then she instructed Ophelia to lie—about being an orphan, about being a gifted student, everything! And that information, Star Darlings, came from Ophelia herself.

And that, finally, brings me to the real purpose of this holo-letter.

The Real Purpose of This Holo-Letter

Why did I write it? Scarlet, Tessa, and I have decided to explore the Star Caves, deep beneath our school. We are looking for clues in the very labyrinth Lady Stella introduced us to—clues about the headmistress, clues about our missions, clues about anything and everything. (Yes, Gemma, your sister, Tessa, is with us, even though she just came back from her mission and is not a fan of dark, dank, spooky places.)

I have a feeling something big will come out of our search. We are just now setting off. But if you are reading this, it means we have not made it back. We are still underground, in the tunnels, maybe trapped and most definitely in trouble. So . . . help! Find us as fast as you can!

Yours in jeopardy,
Cassie

CHAPTER
1

"*Mmmmmm, hmmmm, mmmm, hmmmm.*" Adora hummed tunelessly, alone in her dorm room.

It felt nice to have the room all to herself. Still, it was a little strange that Tessa, her roommate, wasn't there.

The two had just come back from a Wish Mission. It was Tessa's mission; Adora had yet to be chosen for her own mission to Wishworld. But Adora had been sent to help when the situation looked dim. Really, Tessa had been so caught up in her Wisher's emotions that she hadn't been able to see the orchard for the ozziefruit trees. Luckily, Adora had set her straight. So thank the stars, the trip had been successful and quite exciting.

After the Star Darlings ceremony, where Tessa had

gotten her Power Crystal, Adora had expected her to come straight back to their room. Tessa was quite the homebody, after all. And there were her virtual galliope, Jewel, to feed and her micro-zap waiting to bake yummy astromuffins.

But Tessa hadn't so much as stopped off at the room as far as Adora could tell. She was probably catching up with her younger sister, Gemma. And Adora planned to take full advantage of her alone time.

She had been right in the middle of an experiment when she'd been called on to help Tessa. She'd been itching to get back to it for over a starday now. It combined her two biggest passions: science and fashion—specifically sequins.

Adora wanted the sequins to be extra twinkly. That alone wouldn't be so difficult. But she wanted that newfound sparkle to bring out each sequin's color, too, to make the shades themselves brighter, warmer, and more radiant.

The gold sequins Leona favored had to become even more brightly golden; Cassie's silvery pink ones even more silvery pink; Clover's an even deeper, more brilliant purple. And Adora's goal was to do it with just one formula.

She wanted the formula to work with every shade under the suns, and that was twelve in the Star Darlings group alone. Add all the different tones at Starling Academy, or, furthermore, all of Starland itself, and the numbers were starmazing!

Adora had already removed natural elements from glittery yellow calliope flowers, fiery red florafierces, and other plants and trees. Now she needed to add twinkle-oxide—with a spark of glowzene for good measure—to each mixture. The combination had to be just right so the formula would react with any Starling shade.

Luckily, it was Reliquaday, the first starday of the weekend, which gave her plenty of time to test her ideas. Adora would be logical and methodical, as always. But she wanted to get it done sooner rather than later so the sequins could be sewn onto outfits the Star Darlings band members planned to wear for the upcoming Battle of the Bands on Starshine Day.

"*Mmmmm, hmmm, mmmmm.*" Adora hummed, pouring 5.6 lumins of twinkle-oxide into a beaker. "*Mmmm, hmmmmm.*" She turned on her personal bright-burner to 179 degrees Starrius and waited for the mixture to heat. "*Mmmm.*"

Alone in the room, Adora felt free to sing to her heart's content. Her music skills were nothing to brag about, but Adora wasn't much into the arts, anyway. For her, it was science, science, science—and fashion, fashion, fashion.

Adora planned to be a style scientist, maybe the first on all of Starland. And she'd show everyone she could be the brightest in both style and science.

Adora's parents owned a trendy clothing store in Radiant Hills, the ultraexclusive community in Starland City where Libby had grown up alongside glimmerous celebrighties and famous Starlandians.

Adora herself had lived in a perfectly nice neighborhood of modest, comfortable homes. She couldn't complain. She and her parents had shared a simple one-level house where they each had their own workspace to create designs to sell in the store. Even as a wee Starling, she'd had a microscope and a star-sewing machine and had come up with lustrous new fabrics for her parents to use in their clothing designs.

Adora pushed back sky-blue strands of hair that had fallen out of her loose bun, and adjusted her knee-length glittery lab coat and gloves. She checked her pockets, making sure the extra test tubes she always carried around were closed up tight.

Finally, with great care, she straightened her safety starglasses. Safety first, she knew from prior experience.

Just this staryear, Tessa had mixed a batch of glorange smoothies. Adora, meanwhile, had been working on special fabric that would sparkle extra brightly when it got wet. She'd combined orangey lightning in a bottle with starfuric acid and was ready to soak the fabric. The mixture did look a bit like the smoothies, Adora had to admit. So it was no wonder Tessa had reached for the wrong container and lifted it to her lips, about to take a sip. Adora had to make a running dive to knock the liquid out of her hands.

Right after that, Adora had established rules, including clearly separating food from experiments and wearing safety starglasses. The second one was particularly important, Adora realized a starsec later, when—

Bang! Her sequin mixture fizzled and sparked, overflowing from the beaker and spilling onto her workspace. Immediately, the smoking liquid disappeared, thanks to the self-cleaning technology featured in all Starland dwellings.

Adora's side of the room in particular was squeaky clean and spare—some might say sterile and uninteresting—with a neat desktop and lab space containing carefully arranged beakers and test tubes. Even the "fashion section" had neat cubbies for bolts of fabrics and a carefully polished star-sewing machine.

She did like an orderly room, with minimal possessions. Tessa, on the other hand, had a moonium knickknacks—along with plants and herbs and old holo-cookbooks.

Adora didn't quite understand. She didn't get attached to things. *Out with the old, in with the new,* she thought frequently, deleting old experiment notes and equations. She was thinking that now, in fact, as she struck the sequins formula from her holo–lab notes.

"*Starf,*" Adora said, eying the now blank screen. She'd have to start over, maybe lowering the bright-burner to 147 degrees. But that was okay. That was what science was all about—trial and error and patience.

And that was all part of the lightentific method, Adora's personal approach to experimenting: Ask a question based on observation. Come up with a reasonable hypothesis (a guess, really) to answer the question. Create an experiment to see if the guess was correct and analyze the results. Finally, draw a conclusion. Either the experiment worked or it failed.

But Adora wasn't one to accept failure.

"*Mmmmmm.*" Adora's voice grew more powerful as

she started on a new hypothesis. It was a relief, really, to be loud. She had been so frustrated when no one had been able to hear her for so long, only later realizing the poisonous nail polish was causing her to whisper. At least it had been better than giggling nonstop, like Sage, though. Or pulling practical jokes, like Astra had done. No one liked it when their drinks were switched at the Celestial Café!

Adora was carefully carrying fresh batches of the mixture to the bright-burner when her Star-Zap buzzed.

Should she ignore it and just keep concentrating on her experiment?

Part of her wanted to do just that. But with all the strange goings-on lately, it could be an important message. Or maybe it was an announcement for the next mission!

"Oh, moonberries," she said, using Tessa's favorite expression as she set down the beakers. She'd just have to check. She reached for her Star-Zap and glanced at the screen.

A group holo-letter from Cassie? she thought. That was a little bizarre. Why would Cassie write a long letter when she could just talk to the Star Darlings or send a brief holo-text?

Adora tapped the screen and the letter appeared in

the air, floating at eye level. Quickly, she read the note, then read it again just to be sure: Cassie was with Tessa—and Scarlet—and they were trapped in the Star Caves. There Adora was, happily going about her experiment, pleased as sparkle-punch to have the room to herself, while Tessa had been in trouble the whole time.

Every problem had a solution—scientific, mathematical, or otherwise. It just took a cool, clear mind to figure it out. But Adora had to leave the room, step away from Tessa's knickknacks and holo-photos from the farm, to think things through. Calmly, she went outside.

"Adora! Thank the stars you're here!" Leona shouted, rushing down the hall, her golden curls bouncing behind her. "Did you see Cassie's holo-letter?"

"Shhh!" hissed Adora. She glanced pointedly in the other direction, where two third years were getting off the Cosmic Transporter and eyeing them curiously.

"Just the SDs being SDish," one said with a laugh.

Ask just about any Starling Academy student and she would say *SD* stood for *Slow Developers*, a nickname given to the twelve girls because they all attended a special class for extra help. Little did the students know, however, that *SD* was short for *Star Darlings*. And the "extra help" was lessons in information about Wishworld that they used on actual Wish Missions.

Adora shrugged off the label and the idea that anyone would think she was a weak student. It just went to show you how dim other Starlings could be, she thought. Particularly those girls still hanging around the hall, trying to eavesdrop on her conversation with Leona.

"We should all get together to talk about the holo-letter," she told Leona. "Right now."

"Must be an SD assignment," one of the eavesdropping girls said. "A sloooow assignment." Happy with their insults, the girls moved on.

"Of course," said Leona in a calmer voice. "I'll holo-text everyone right away. We should meet in my room. It's the perfect place. You know I have my own personal stage? So it's all set for a group discussion. Whoever wants to talk can use the microphone."

"Right," said Adora, though she didn't think they really needed a microphone. What they needed was a plan.

CHAPTER
2

Adora was sitting crisscross starapple sauce, as they used to say in Wee Constellation School. Most of the Star Darlings gathered in Leona's room sat the same way. Of course, Piper went one better, putting her feet *on top* of the opposite legs and placing her hands palms-up in a meditative pose. It wasn't the most comfortable position, Adora knew.

She'd actually tried it when she'd joined Piper in a meditation class. She'd wanted to test the effectiveness of being in the moment, of being aware of each movement. Adora had left with a healthy respect for mindful thinking—and sore legs.

The girls were grouped around Leona's mini star-shaped stage, waiting while Leona searched for her microphone. "I know it's here somewhere!" Leona shouted, flinging starbrushes, shoes, and accessories everywhere.

The room was bathed in a golden light, filtering through gauzy starlight curtains. Adora couldn't help wondering if she could capture that exact shade for Leona's sequins.

Adora's eyes swept over the other Star Darlings, and she noted their coloring. Sweet-looking Libby, with her jellyjooble-pink hair, leaned forward worriedly. Sleepy Piper half closed her seafoam-green eyes.

Fiery red-haired Astra—a perfect match for the florafierce extract, Adora realized—dusted off her star ball uniform.

"You know, I got Cassie's message right in the middle of the Glowin' Glions star ball game," she was saying to Piper, "and when I was leaving, I spotted Leebeau in the stands!"

Adora frowned. She'd heard about that boy, Astra's "biggest fan," who went to Star Preparatory, the school across Luminous Lake. Astra had met him on a starbus, on the way to visit an orphanage during the search for the missing Ophelia. And she'd been keeping an eye out for him in the stands at every game since.

There might be some scientific explanation for

Astra's interest in the boy. That would be fascinating to pursue. But it didn't quite figure into Adora's game plan.

"So he's finally here," Astra continued, "and I had to leave! And miss the rest of the game!"

Piper nodded sympathetically. "If you're destined to see him again, it will happen."

Surprisingly, Astra nodded. "It's true. This is an emergency situation."

"Yes!" Adora agreed, standing to address the group. "So what are we going to do about it?"

"Ahem!" Leona cleared her throat, hurrying over. "I found the microphone." She tapped it to make her point, and the thudding sound echoed loudly. "If anyone wants to speak, just signal me and I'll give you the mic."

"Just wait a starsec, Leona," Adora said. "We can't start yet. Where's Gemma?"

Just then, there was a knock at the door. Leona opened it from across the room with a flick of her wrist, and Gemma bounded inside.

"I can't believe Tessa would do this!" she cried, her ginger eyes flashing. "Going down into those creepy caves? If I went down there, she'd be saying, 'It's too dangerous, Gemma. You need to be careful, Gemma. What were you thinking, Gemma?'" Glittery orange tears trickled down Gemma's cheeks. "I'm so worried about Tessa. About them all! What were they thinking? What were—"

"Star excuse me, Gemma," Leona interrupted. "I have the stage . . . I mean, floor . . . I mean, microphone. And we need to begin a real discussion, now that we're all here—except for Cassie, Tessa, and Scarlet, of course."

Scarlet and Leona were roommates. They were a combustible mix, worse than sparkle-oxide and phenol-twinkle. And while Adora and Tessa had their differences, those two definitely did not get along.

As if on cue, Scarlet's skateboard slid down her ramp-like wall, rolled across the room to Leona's side, and came to rest right by the stage.

Piper gasped. "It's a sign. We need to hurry up and do something. Scarlet needs us!"

Sage nodded vigorously. "Yes! Why are we sitting around like a bunch of Starlings in their twilight years?" She jumped up impatiently. "Let's go."

Gemma was already halfway out the door.

"Whoa," said Adora. "Slow down, you two. We all want to find our friends. But we need to approach this methodically and thoughtfully, not like a bunch of bloombugs during a full moon."

Vega nodded, her short blue hair bobbing. "That's

right. It's like a puzzle. We need to fill in the missing pieces to see the whole picture. We know they went down hoping to find some clues about Lady Stella. Now they're in trouble. We need to rescue them." She paused. "And here's the missing piece: how?"

"The only way I know down to the Star Caves is through the secret passage in Lady Stella's office," Astra mused aloud.

The girls exchanged nervous glances. Adora paced back and forth, thinking.

Some professors would have access to the office: Lady Stella's inner circle, those teachers who knew about the Star Darlings and gave special lectures to their class, for instance. But no school visitor—no matter how glimmerous, no matter how famous, no matter how important—was allowed into Lady Stella's office without her personal invitation. As for students, it was strictly forbidden. Bot-Bot guards roamed those halls at all starhours.

Adora didn't know what would happen if a student was caught. Would she be expelled? Refused admittance to any other school? She didn't want to find out.

"Let's analyze this," Adora said out loud. "Maybe the girls didn't go down through Lady Stella's office. Maybe they found another way. Does anyone have thoughts on that?"

Leona spoke into the mic. "Scarlet."

"What?" said Sage. "What does that even mean?"

"It means," Leona continued, "that she's always been fascinated by the caves. From the very first time we went down, Scarlet couldn't wait to go back. Whenever we got a holo-text that a Wish Orb was ready, her glow would flare with excitement. Honestly, I've seen her smile more in those caves than just about anywhere else. She might have found another way down there."

"Once, Scarlet went left when everyone else was going right," Astra added. "I grabbed her arm, thinking that she just wasn't paying attention. But maybe there's something more there. Maybe she was trying to explore on her own."

"Hmmm." Adora pondered the idea. "I believe she does enjoy the caves. I noticed a bitbat land on her shoulder one time, and she actually petted it. So maybe she has gone down on her own before, most likely through a different entrance." Adora shook her head, clearing her thoughts. "But we don't have time to waste trying to find it. I think we are going to have to go down there the only way we know—through Lady Stella's office. So how do you propose we get inside?"

"Well, we certainly can't ask Lady Stella," said Leona. "She's probably the one who trapped them!"

Adora looked around the circle. Astra tapped her foot, shooting off sparks of nervous energy. Gemma chewed on a fingernail. Even Piper had shifted into a tense, upright position.

"Listen," Adora said calmly. "There's a chance this has nothing to do with sabotage or anyone purposefully trapping them."

"That's right," Clover said. She tipped her ever-present purple fedora in a hats-off gesture to Adora. "They might have gotten lost and now they can't find a way out. That would be scary for them, sure, but not very dangerous.

"My family is so big I once got left behind and no one even realized it! We were traveling from New Prism to Solar Springs with the circus, and I was getting supplies for our star-swallowing act when the circus swift train took off without me. My uncle Octavius had to teleport back to pick me up."

Adora always found Clover's circus stories interesting. (The Flying Molensas not only used scientific equations to figure out trapeze trajectories; they also wore starmazing outfits.) But right now they needed to focus on the task at hand: rescuing their friends.

"So we need to come up with a plan to get into Lady

Stella's office," she said out loud. "Without getting caught."

"I think we should choose a leader," Libby added. "Someone to be in charge."

"So we don't have endless discussions," Clover cracked, "like this one."

"Like a team captain!" Astra said eagerly.

"Or light leader," Libby told the group. Everyone knew that she intended to run for class office one day. "I say we take a vote."

"I nominate Leona!" said Leona.

"You can't nominate yourself!" Astra exclaimed. "But if someone would like to nominate me, I think I could do a starmendous job. I understand group dynamics and winning, and—"

"How about we don't nominate anyone and just all vote anonymously?" said Adora. She quickly set up a survey site on her Star-Zap, then made a few adjustments for the group to vote.

Immediately, everyone tapped in their responses. Only Adora waited, thinking for more than a starmin. She considered Astra first, then Libby—who had shown leadership by suggesting the election—then everyone else equally. But in the end, weighing all the evidence, she clicked on a checkmark next to her own name.

Libby did a quick tally. "Adora!" she announced.

"Starkudos," said Astra quickly. "You'll make a great leader."

Adora hadn't really expected to win. Those things tended to be popularity contests. Sure, Adora thought she was popular in her own way. After a hard day's work at the lab, she liked to socialize as much as the next Starling. But that didn't mean she had many close friends.

Adora was certain that a good number of Starlings thought she could be a little cold and unfeeling. But she disagreed. She was just calm and logical. She didn't let feelings get in the way of decisions. And apparently, that was the best approach right then.

"You won't be sorry," she told everyone.

"I know," said Gemma, reaching out to touch her hand. "You'll get everything under control."

Adora nodded. "But I don't want to be the lone voice."

"Surely *my* voice should be heard," said Leona. She grinned graciously. "Even if this time I'm only a backup singer."

"All right," said Adora. "I propose another vote. Should I choose one or two girls to go with me down to the caves? Or should we all go together?"

That time, no vote was necessary. Everyone shouted, almost in unison: "Together!"

Adora looked at Astra and grinned. "Let's do this the Glowin' Glions' way."

Everyone moved onto the stage, drawing closer and placing their hands in the center of the group, one on top of the other.

"But instead of a team name," Adora continued, "let's say—"

She didn't even have to finish the sentence.

"Star Darlings!" they all cried.

CHAPTER
3

Quickly, Adora reviewed the situation. So far the Star Darlings had decided:

1) to make the rescue a group effort, and
2) to sneak into Lady Stella's office to take the secret entrance to the Star Caves.

Now she had to put her lightentific method to use.

Generally, she would start by thinking, *If I did A, then B, I'd most likely get C.*

First she sent a scout to Lady Stella's office to see if she was there. The result was inconclusive. Rather than take a chance that the headmistress was inside, Adora came up with a plan. In this case, her hypothesis was:

(A) If we make sure Lady Stella is not in her office, we could (B) sneak inside and open the secret entrance and (C) rescue Cassie, Tessa, and Scarlet.

Step One: determining Lady Stella's location.

Of course, there had to be a conclusion at the end of the whole process, an answer to the bigger questions: Had the girls been trapped on purpose? And by whom? But Adora thought those questions would have to wait. First things first, and the first thing in this case was the rescue.

Everyone was still in Leona's room, looking at Adora expectantly. "Okay," she told them in a firm voice. "We'll divide into pairs to scout around for Lady Stella."

Her eyes settled on Libby. "Libby," she said. "You come with me. Everyone else, find a partner."

While the others milled around, Adora took out her Star-Zap and opened a holo-map of Starling Academy. The school was in the shape of a five-point star, with the Little Dipper and Big Dipper Dorms clustered in one point. Faculty housing was in the point to their right, at the very tip. *Libby and I will go there*, Adora decided. *Now, how far should the others spread out?*

She peered at the holo-map intently. She was so absorbed in the task that she didn't notice someone standing next to her until she felt a tap on her shoulder.

"Um, Adora?" said Gemma. "I don't have a partner." She blinked rapidly, trying to hold back tears.

Adora stared at her, uncomprehending. The girl was overwrought. She needed to get in control.

Of course Adora realized Gemma was upset about her sister. But really, it did no good going into a star-tizzy. Besides, Gemma should have been the first to pair up; the girl never hesitated to approach anyone and start chattering away.

For stars' sake, if it was me, Adora thought, *I'd be just as happy to work alone. In fact, it would be easier.* Already she half regretted having Libby come with her. She'd just tell Libby and Gemma to go together.

"Gemma," she said, "you and Libby—"

"Can go with you!" Gemma's face lit up. "Oh, star salutations, Adora! I'll just run to the Lightning Lounge and scrounge up some snacks before we go. I know Tessa will be hungry!"

Before Adora could stop her, Gemma was gone.

Adora sighed. This was going to be a long step one.

Not long after, the Star Darlings dispersed, each pair heading in a different direction. Adora had assigned Astra and Sage the Radiant Recreation Center and the surrounding area; Piper and Vega the Illumination Library and classrooms in Halo Hall; and Leona and Clover the band shell, the Celestial Café, and the nearby orchard.

She'd told everyone to set their Star-Zaps for reminders to meet at the hedge maze in precisely one half starhour.

Vega had nodded in agreement. "The hedge maze is perfect," she'd told the others. "It's a great place to meet in secret."

Stepping onto the Cosmic Transporter, Gemma linked arms with Adora and Libby. "Come on," she urged. "We were the last to leave, so we need to hurry!"

Adora didn't bother to remind Gemma why they were last: she and Libby had had to wait for her to get back with ozziefruit and astromuffins. But teacher housing wasn't too far away, so they hadn't lost much startime.

Just starmins later, the three girls hopped off the transporter and found themselves in front of a small holo-sign. The flowing print read simply FACULTY.

If Adora hadn't been looking for some sort of sign, she might have missed it. There was nothing else to indicate there were homes there.

Adora saw boingtrees and druderwomp bushes, along with the Crystal Mountains in the background, looming beyond Luminous Lake. That was all. But Adora knew for a fact that teachers lived there. It said so right on the sign, not to mention the map. Indisputable proof. But she'd never actually been to that part of campus before. It was all new to her.

"This is odd. Where are all the houses?" she asked. "Have either of you been to a professor's home?"

Libby and Gemma shook their heads. "We're only first years," Gemma reminded her. "Don't older students usually get invited for twinkle tea? I thought by third year everyone had been here at least once."

Adora hoped Gemma would stop at that, but unsurprisingly, she continued talking. "I know Tessa has been here a bunch of times. She never made it seem like a top secret location. All the other third years talk about their visits. Have you at least been invited, Adora?"

Adora almost blushed an icy blue. But she didn't. By sheer force of will, she held herself in check. "I meet with teachers all the time. After class. In the Astro-Energy Lab. Or the Sparkle-Transfer Space. I just don't have time for twinkle tea or leisurely conversation."

Adora realized she hadn't quite answered Gemma's question. If she had, she would have said, *No, I've never been invited.* She had her theories about why. The science teachers thought she was too frivolous, too interested in clothes and fashion. And the art teachers thought she was too factual and serious-minded to discuss painting and wish-energy sculpting. Besides, she told herself, she wanted her grades to reflect her work, not her student-teacher relationships.

She paused, frowning. "It never occurred to me it would be hard to find."

Now Adora did blush. She usually had all contingencies covered, all what-ifs thought out. Not knowing what else to do, she stepped forward to examine the sign. Finally, she noticed the hand scanner on a nearby boingtree.

Is this area open to all students? she wondered. *Or do you need special permission?* Would her palm open some sort of door?

Adora groaned. How could she have been on campus for three years and not know any of that?

Well, there was only one way to find out. She placed her hand on the scanner, and it glowed blue. Directly ahead of the girls, shimmery leaves parted like a curtain to reveal a small suburban neighborhood.

Homes of all colors, shapes, and sizes circled a village green. Lampposts, bright rainbows arcing from them, bordered the green.

"Why do these houses look so familiar?" Libby asked.

Adora gazed intently at the homes. Libby was right. There was something about this place . . . something recognizable that made her feel she'd seen it before. Maybe she'd been somewhere similar . . . seen the houses in some other form . . .

She snapped her fingers. "I've got it!" she cried. She pointed at a stunning umber-colored home with silver-white trim and long elegant lines. It seemed so inviting, so warm and open, Adora wanted to walk right inside. "Does that remind you of anyone?" she asked.

Libby smiled. "Professor Eugenia Bright!"

Professor Eugenia Bright taught Wish Fulfillment. She was so lovely and welcoming—just like the house— that Starlings signed up for her classes starmester after starmester.

"And that must be Professor Dolores Raye's right next to it," said Adora.

That home was small, tidy, and off-putting, with a sign that read KEEP OFF THE STARGRASS.

Windows flanked its front door so it resembled a face with large-framed glasses perched on its "nose." And it seemed, Adora had to admit, like a boring place to live.

"It looks just like her!" Gemma giggled. Unlike Professor Eugenia Bright's lectures, Professor Dolores Raye's Wishful Thinking class—covering the nuts and bolts of wish energy manipulation—was cut-and-dried, all business with little spark.

"And guess who lives there!" Adora pointed to a short, squat home that gave the impression it was falling apart. Shutters hung slightly askew, and wispy purple grass escaped the confines of the yard, like hair from a bun.

Suddenly, the front door swung open. The girls all jumped as Lady Cordial stepped outside, checking her Star-Zap and hurrying as if she'd just received an important message.

Z-z-z-z. Adora's own Star-Zap buzzed at the same time. She gave it a quick look, already knowing it was a holo-reminder to meet the Star Darlings at the hedge maze.

Just then, Lady Cordial tripped over a glimmervine. Her purse fell to the ground, and all its contents spilled onto the walkway.

Libby rushed to help. "Lady Cordial! Let me get those things for you!"

"Oh, my s-s-s-s-stars," Lady Cordial stuttered. "What are you girls doing here?" She stooped down to gather her things, accidentally knocking Libby farther away.

Adora bent down to help.

"No! I can do it myself!" exclaimed Lady Cordial. Clearly, she was embarrassed by her clumsiness.

"Star greetings, students and teacher!" Professor Findley Claxworth was fast approaching. His long, loose paint-splattered smock swung in the breeze. His lavender eyes, a perfect match for his hair and glasses, twinkled merrily.

Everyone liked the affable art professor. Adora had taken his Aspirational Art classes—Introduction to, Advanced, and Exceptionally Advanced. She liked him, too. But she feared he was one of the teachers who thought she spent too much startime focused on the scientific end of art and design.

Professor Findley Claxworth smiled warmly. "Ladies," he said, including the Star Darlings in the greeting.

Libby's and Gemma's glows deepened with pleasure.

"Star greetings, Professor Findley Claxworth," said Adora.

Lady Cordial barely nodded, too busy closing her purse and clucking in embarrassment at her clumsiness.

"To what do we owe the pleasure of your company?" he asked the girls.

Gemma and Libby stepped back to let Adora take over.

"We're tracking flutterfocuses for my Comparative Creatures class. I think they flew over here. Libby and Gemma are just helping me." Adora was lying, and Libby and Gemma knew it. She only hoped Lady Cordial and Professor Findley Claxworth didn't.

Adora rarely lied, and she doubted she was very good at it. As a scientist, Adora believed in truth and accuracy—both in experiments in the lab and in life outside the lab. How could she consider herself a true scientist—not to mention a good Starling—if she allowed facts to be altered to fit her own needs?

But every once in a while, it needed to be done.

"That's interesting," said Lady Cordial distractedly. "I didn't notice any s-s-s-s-swarms. But I've been inside most of the day, going through admissions applications. Next s-s-s-s-staryear's incoming class looks like a s-s-s-s-strong one."

"Oh!" Gemma piped up, suddenly interested. "Are there any applications from Solar Springs, my hometown?"

Adora felt sure Lady Cordial wouldn't give out that kind of confidential information unless it was by accident. She was too thoughtful and by-the-holo-book. But Adora knew the sweetly bumbling head of admissions was certainly capable of slipping up. To save her any more embarrassment, Adora turned to Professor Findley Claxworth and changed the subject. "Are you working on something right now?"

"Why, star salutations for asking, Adora," he said, clearly pleased. "I'm just about to start my new piece. And I'm thrilled to have an audience."

He waved his arms, and a small white house that looked like a blank canvas built on easel-like stilts lit up with a soft glow. Adora noted the neat garden in front. Then she realized the flowers were really lightpaint cans.

Professor Findley Claxworth snapped his fingers and the cans rose into the air. He pointed to one. It swung back and forth, splashing bright yellow lightpaint against one side of the house. He snapped again and the other cans flung vibrant blues and greens. He fluttered his fingers and the dripping lightpaint transformed into a field of bluebeezel flowers under setting suns.

"S-s-s-s-so lovely," Lady Cordial stammered.

"Just experimenting," Professor Findley Claxworth said modestly.

Experimenting! Adora had to focus on her own light-entific method. They had to find out if Lady Stella was home.

"And I'm just leaving." Lady Cordial interrupted

Adora's thoughts. "S-s-s-s-star apologies, girls. Next time you visit, I'll have you over for twinkle tea and astro-muffins." With one final nod, she disappeared through the leaves.

"Anyone like to try another side of the house?" Professor Findley Claxworth asked. "I have plenty of lightpaint left."

"Yes!" said Libby and Gemma, stepping forward.

"Yes, we'd all love to try," Adora said firmly, "but we have to find those flutterfocuses!" She turned to Gemma. "*Tessa* is in my Comparative Creatures class," she added, stressing Tessa's name. "She needs this information, too."

"Of course!" Gemma's eyes flashed. Her voice rose in agitation. "Tessa! The project! We don't have time for anything else!"

Suddenly, silence descended, as if a blanket had been thrown over Starling Academy, muffling all sound. The distant whir of the Cosmic Transporter, the faraway hum of the startrack, all the regular every-starday noise—the kind you didn't notice until it ceased—stopped. The light of the rainbow lamps shut off with a click.

The Starlings stared at the lampposts in disbelief. Another energy outage! They'd been happening more and more frequently.

"One, two, three . . ." Adora counted the starsecs, and at twenty-seven, the lights blinked back on.

"Really just a blip!" said Professor Findley Claxworth almost cheerfully. "And it helped me see my painting in a different light. It definitely needs a hint of purple to balance the colors more—" Then he seemed to catch himself. "Of course, these blackouts are terrible. Just terrible."

He smiled once more at the girls. "I hope to see you all in my next starmester classes. Adora, look into Art of Wishing. It's a high-level elective!" And he slipped inside his house.

Gemma grabbed Adora's arm. "Oh, my stars! Did you hear him? The professor actually likes the outages! He could be behind the energy shortage, the one who's trying to mess up our missions."

Libby gasped. "Maybe he thinks we'd all create more art if Starland ran out of energy! If we didn't have Star-Zaps or transporters or swift trains, we'd all slow down and really look at things." She shook her head, confused. "Not that it would be bad to focus on art."

"Let's not think about good or bad, or why or why not," Adora said. "And let's not jump to conclusions! We can discuss art versus science all starday long when Starland is on track again."

She paused to check her Star-Zap. They really had to leave. They'd spent way too much time there already, and the other Star Darlings might be waiting.

"But right now, let's find Lady Stella's house."

CHAPTER
4

Adora led the two younger Starlings around the village green to look at the row of houses facing the Crystal Mountains. She kept her eyes open for the headmistress's house. Lady Stella had a classic kind of beauty. She wasn't flashy—not like that globe-shaped house with hydrongs of stars shooting out the chimney. Or that hot-pink one with bright yellow shutters opening and closing as if it was rapidly blinking.

Lady Stella was stately; she moved in a calm, unhurried way. Adora had admired her from the starmin they'd met. She couldn't really be guilty of sabotage, could she? That would be truly devastating.

Something caught in Adora's throat.

Odd, thought Adora. *Am I coming down with star pox?*

She pushed the possibility out of her mind and concentrated on Lady Stella.

She'd been reserving judgment on the headmistress, determined not to brand her innocent or guilty until all the evidence was in and the findings were incontrovertible. Still, thinking about Lady Stella's powerful, dignified presence made Adora long for her to be innocent.

One olive-colored house caught her eye. It stood in a far corner, tucked between two rare and beautiful kaleidoscope trees that were constantly shifting colors. Its lines were simple yet elegant, its color understated but glowing. A calm golden-white light radiated from its windows.

"That must be it," she whispered. Libby and Gemma nodded.

Adora took a holo-pad out of her coat pocket and quickly sketched a flutterfocus. "This can be our cover if we see anyone else," she added.

"On the farm, Tessa always chased flutterfocuses." Gemma began to prattle, as if they were really working on a class project. Adora let her talk as they skirted other houses. But when they drew closer to Lady Stella's home, she held up a hand for silence. Then she pulled them behind a kaleidoscope tree.

"Hush. We need to be quiet now. Lady Stella knows too much about our classes and homework for the flutter-focuses to work."

She peered through the color-shifting leaves. Lady Stella was nowhere to be seen.

"Are you sure this is her house?" whispered Gemma, beginning to panic once again.

"*Shhh!* Do you hear that?" Adora hissed. Straining to listen, they caught the faint *click-clack* sounds of snipping scissors.

"It's coming from the backyard," Libby said in a low voice.

The three girls nodded at one another. Then they crept along the side of the house until they reached a corner. Peering around, they saw Lady Stella.

She was standing in front of a large, lovely garden ringed by goldenella trees. Glittery yellow calliopes mixed with orange chatterbursts. Coral-colored roxy-linda flowers twined around the purple zelda blooms. Glitterbees buzzed between rows, and a sweet fragrance wafted through the air.

A glowzen pairs of scissors hovered near Lady Stella, as if at rest.

Lady Stella sipped from a tall glass of sparkle juice. Then she waved one arm at the scissors. The scissors seemed to bow, then flew from flower to flower, snipping off brittle leaves.

Lady Stella worked at a leisurely pace, directing the scissors while more tools hovered nearby, ready to work. Clearly, the gardening had just begun.

"The garden is huge," Libby whispered. "This could take a very long time."

Adora agreed. "Lady Stella won't be going to her office at all this afternoon. We need to tell the others. To the hedge maze!"

"Okay, who had the bright idea to meet here?" asked Gemma, pouting a bit.

Adora, who was standing next to Gemma in front of the maze, held back a smile. "It was me. Bet you wish you had paired with Vega now."

Somehow, Vega always knew her way around the maze. A world-class puzzle solver, she actually enjoyed taking tests and figuring out answers. Adora had tried to get Vega's input on an experiment or two over the staryears, but Vega had made it clear she didn't like the guesswork involved. She liked tried-and-true answers, resolutions that had been studied for eons.

"Don't worry," Adora said, trying to reassure

Gemma and Libby, neither of whom had spent much time in the hedge maze. "We'll find our way sooner or later. It's all a matter of trial and error."

Linking arms with the younger Starlings, Adora led them through the maze entrance.

Inside, the tall hedges seemed to tower even higher. It was impossible to gauge location or get a sense of direction. Paths curved this way and that, twisting and turning at every step.

Should we go right? Adora wondered. *Or left? Forward? Or back?*

It didn't matter that she'd visited just the other star-week and had found her way in two shakes of a glion's tail. The maze changed constantly. One starday you could guess correctly and walk straight to the center. But the next, the same path would take you stars knew where. At least with the Glowin' Glions game going on that day, it would most likely be empty.

Star-Zap mapping functions didn't work there, and not everyone enjoyed the challenge. If you panicked— like Gemma was about to, Adora guessed—you could pick one of the red flowers that were placed strategically on every wall and open an exit.

Adora, Gemma, and Libby wandered aimlessly, Gemma growing more fidgety with every dead end.

"Let's head back to the entrance and start over," Adora said, turning everyone around. The next thing she knew, they were standing in the center of the maze.

Vega and Piper were already there.

Piper was relaxing in a comfy lounge chair with a headrest of soft pillows. She reached into a deep pocket of her long flowing dress and took out a sleep mask.

Why does she always carry sleep masks? Adora wondered. *Why close your eyes to the worlds when a universe of possibilities stands right in front of you?*

Vega, meanwhile, sat stick-straight on a stone bench, staring at them with a relieved expression.

"You're finally here!" she cried, jumping up. "Piper and I have been here so long she's falling asleep."

"Not quite," said Piper, taking off the mask. "I'm just using the time to regroup." She turned to Adora. "I'm getting a strong vibe: the others are close by."

Vega hurried toward the path. "I'll poke around and see if I can find them. Be back in a starsec."

Adora had barely settled into a seat when Vega returned with the rest of the Star Darlings.

Leona flung herself onto the lounge chair, squeezing in next to Piper. "Scoot over, Piper. I need to rest my weary bones." She lifted one foot to examine the sole of her delicate golden sandal. "Scarlet and her combat boots would have done better tramping all over Starling Academy and through this maze. I am so done!"

Piper adjusted a pillow for her. "Star salutations," Leona murmured.

"Don't get too comfortable," Adora warned. "We should move quickly. Lady Stella is busy at home, but—"

"We have to tell you about the faculty housing," Libby said excitedly. "It's so starmazing."

Sage looked at Libby eagerly. Everyone else regarded her with amused expressions. "We've all been there," Astra said.

"Well, how could we be sure?" Gemma asked. "Adora—"

"Let's get back to Lady Stella," Adora said quickly. "She's gardening. I'm not sure when she'll finish. And we don't know who else may be near her office. So we should divide into small groups, again, to avoid suspicion."

She noticed Gemma and Libby edging closer to Vega.

"We'll all leave the maze together," she added. "Vega, you go first."

With Vega leading the way, it took only a starmin to exit the hedge maze. Outside, Adora decided to stay on her own. It seemed simplest; that way she could avoid any complicating opinions or outbursts.

She made a wide circle around Halo Hall, not seeing

a glimmer of another Starling. She thanked her lucky stars for the star ball game. Quickly, Adora ducked into a side entrance. Glancing over her shoulder—still no one in sight—she hurried down a gleaming starmarble hall. She had just turned a corner when she spied Leona and Sage ahead. *Might as well stick together,* she thought, rushing to catch up.

Just as she reached the others, a Bot-Bot swooped over their heads, stopping to block their path.

Adora caught her breath. Was it a security guard?

"Mojo! What are you doing here?" asked Sage.

Mojo? That didn't sound like any Bot-Bot name Adora had ever heard before. Not willing to say anything aloud in case the Bot-Bot was recording, she turned to Sage and raised her eyebrows.

"Oh, Mojo is really MO-J4, but that sounds so . . . um . . . robot-like!" Sage finished. "He was my tour guide when I first came to school. And we've developed a bit of a . . . um, friendship."

The Bot-Bot seemed to smile.

"That's so cute!" said Leona.

To Adora, this was quite startling. All Bot-Bots were polite and—she hoped—programmed to be well meaning. But she'd never seen one with a personality before.

"I'm on security detail," Mojo explained. "Are you

girls here to look for a lost holo-textbook? I spotted a few in the Astral Accounting lecture hall." He winked. "I won't tell your professor. Promise."

"Star salutations!" Adora said before Sage could say a word. "We'll look there right now!" She pulled Sage and Leona down the hall.

"Wait!" called Mojo. "Astral Accounting is the other way."

Adora hit her head. "Of course, you're right!" The three girls turned in the other direction and kept walking until Mojo was gone.

"You didn't need to lie," Sage complained. "Mojo is totally trustworthy."

"You never know," Adora told her. "We need to be careful." Still, it pained Adora to lie once more. Even little light lies went against her scientific, accurate-to-a-fault mindset. But right then it seemed necessary.

Adora glanced around cautiously. "And if there's one Bot-Bot guard, there's bound to be more."

The three girls pressed themselves against the wall, then continued toward Lady Stella's office. The other Star Darlings were quietly moving up behind them as they neared the door.

Adora grinned. *Almost there. Just a few more steps.*

Suddenly, she spied another guard, coming from the opposite direction.

She stopped short. "Oh!" cried Sage, bumping into her from behind. A chorus of "ohs" followed as, one after the other, the still-moving Star Darlings bumped into the ones who'd stopped.

"We're like a clown act from the circus!" Clover joked. Everyone laughed—until they saw the guard.

"What are we going to do?" cried Gemma.

"Calm down and go back around the corner until it's all clear," said Adora. "I'll try to distract it."

As the Bot-Bot neared, Adora slipped away from the others, running up and down halls to make a U-turn and approach the Bot-Bot from behind. She carefully took out the test tubes she was carrying, mixed them together, and threw them against the wall, knowing there would be an explosion.

Bang! It worked!

The Bot-Bot swiveled around. It swooped to the wall, examined the broken glass and liquid mixture, and took a sample before it all disappeared. *Good*, thought Adora. It would take the specimen to the school lab for analysis. That should take some time.

Meanwhile, Adora raced back to Lady Stella's office.

By then the girls were crowded around the door. Each girl placed her hand on the scanner, and each time it beeped and turned red.

Of course the door is locked, Adora told herself sternly. *Why didn't I think of that earlier?* And the Bot-Bot was already back, flying toward them once again. She needed another distraction.

But she'd used up her bag of scientific tricks. Now what?

CHAPTER
5

"Halt!" the Bot-Bot guard called out to the Star Darlings.

In her head, Adora ran through a list of ideas, explanations of why they were there. Then she logically discarded each one. Finally, she had it.

"How about a starring role in 'Fainting on the Floor While Searching for My Homework'?" she whispered to Leona.

"I accept," said Leona.

Quickly, Leona strode to the center of the hall, away from the other Star Darlings, and clutched her head.

"Moons and stars!" she cried. "All of a sudden, I don't feel well. I was trying to find my Astral Accounting holo-textbook . . . but now I don't know where I am. Everything is a blur!"

The Bot-Bot snapped to attention.

Leona staggered farther from the girls—and the door—then collapsed on the floor.

Meanwhile, Adora led the others around the corner to hide.

"Do not worry. I am programmed to aid in emergency situations," said the Bot-Bot tonelessly.

"Please, please," Leona said softly as it hovered above her. "Get help."

"I will not leave you. I will call for more Bot-Bots."

"No!" Leona sat up quickly. Then she realized her mistake and lay back down. "No, please," she whimpered.

"I'll give her a gold star for acting," Adora said, watching from her hiding place.

"I need you to get help," Leona continued. "Make sure the EMBs bring a stretcher. Don't signal them— bring them here so there's no misunderstanding."

That's good, Adora thought. *Getting Emergency Medical Bots might take a while.* Of course, that was what she'd thought about taking the explosive mixture to the lab!

"Bring them . . ." Leona paused. "And my mother."

"Your mother," the Bot-Bot repeated.

Adora clapped a hand over her mouth to keep from laughing.

"Where is your mother located exactly?"

"Probably in the shoe store," Leona gasped.

Adora knew Leona's family worked in the shoe business—not show business. Locating that one tiny shoe store would prove difficult for the guard. Leona really was a starmendous improviser.

"There are no shoe stores in Starling Academy."

"It's in Flairfield."

Adora elbowed Clover. Flairfield was floozels away.

Leona shut her eyes and lay very still, barely breathing.

"Miss?" said the Bot-Bot. "Miss? I am not programmed for these kinds of decisions."

Leona stayed quiet.

The Bot-Bot floated above her uncertainly, then took off in the direction of Health Services.

Immediately, Leona popped to her feet. She met Adora and the others back at the door.

"We don't have much time," Adora whispered loudly. "Who knows when that guard will come back?"

"And what if it actually brings my mother?" Leona added.

Adora didn't answer. She and the others stared at the door. There didn't seem to be much else to do.

As every Starling Academy student knew, individual wish energy manipulation didn't work on locked doors.

Still, Adora thought, they didn't know for a fact that a group of nine advanced students, working together, couldn't open one small locked door.

"Let's try doing this all at once," she suggested. Everyone stared hard at Lady Stella's office door. "On the count of three," she continued. "One, two, and—"

All the Star Darlings focused, seeing in their minds' eyes the door whooshing open.

It didn't move a star inch.

They tried again and the result was conclusive: they couldn't do it.

Astra pulled Adora aside. "When Libby and I were on Wishworld, we got locked out of the auditorium, and she used her Power Crystal to open the door."

Adora rubbed her hands excitedly. "Good thinking," she said. Adora faced the group. "Okay, anyone who has a Power Crystal, take it out now and we'll see what they can do."

Libby, Astra, Sage, Vega, and Piper hurriedly took out their crystals.

"Show-offs," muttered Leona, stepping back.

Get over it! Adora was about to tell her. *So your Wish*

Pendant burned to a crisp while you were coming home after your mission. So you didn't bring back wish energy or receive your Power Crystal. Figure out what you can do now!

Instead, Piper spoke up. "Leona," she said almost sternly, "you should be sending positive thoughts. That could be your way to help."

Adora did believe in positive energy; she'd seen its effects for herself. Once, when her star-sewing machine had some sort of breakdown, she'd visualized it rethreading, concentrated fiercely, and somehow the machine had righted itself.

"Gemma, Clover, and I will add our positive thoughts, too," Adora said. So five Star Darlings placed their Power Crystals on the door while four others sent out positivity vibes.

The door stayed shut.

The girls tried again and again, but each time their energy grew weaker. Finally, they gave up.

"Well," said Leona, "guess those little old Power Crystals aren't as powerful as you thought."

"You're right," said Adora dejectedly. *Why do the Power Crystals work on Wishworld, but not on Starland?* she wondered. *That is very curious.* She examined the door one last time, just to make sure. It was still closed tightly.

She gazed out the window and saw a group of Bot-Bots heading toward the building entrance. They carried a stretcher.

"The EMBs are here," she told the others. "We need to leave and come up with another plan."

She heard a noise, a soft thud of some sort, close behind them. She whirled around to see Leona giggling—in front of the open door!

"How did you do that?" she asked.

"I leaned on it and it slid open!" said Leona.

"This way," the guard called to the other Bot-Bots. "The student is around the corner."

Adora peered inside the office. "It's empty," she whispered. "Hurry!"

Quickly, the girls slipped inside and closed the door behind them.

"Where is the student in distress?" one EMB asked in a level voice. On the other side of the door, Adora raised a finger to her lips, signaling the others to keep quiet.

"I do not know," said the guard.

There was the sound of some movement. Maybe the EMBs were putting down the stretcher to search the area.

"She was here just a few starmins ago," the guard added.

"GR-D3," the EMB said, "you just returned from a technical support appointment, did you not?"

"Maybe," said the guard.

"You cannot even answer that. Clearly your rewiring tune-up was faulty."

"Yes," the guard agreed. "Star excuse my false report." Then there was silence.

"They left," Adora whispered. She glanced around the office. There was the familiar silver table, where they'd gathered many times for Star Darlings meetings.

There were the huge picture windows and the holo-bookcase. And there were the other Star Darlings, of course. But the room seemed empty without Lady Stella. It was uncomfortable—maybe even wrong, Adora considered. It was almost a lie to be there without permission, and it was strange not to have Cassie, Tessa, and Scarlet with them.

The girls stood close together in the center of the room. They looked at one another guiltily. Gemma gripped Adora's hand, her face flushed orange with fear and concern.

"It's all right," Adora said calmly. "But let's not linger. There's the desk."

Of course everyone knew the desk was there. Everyone knew it had a secret drawer, with a button to open a hidden door, the entrance to the Star Caves. Adora just felt she had to say something to get everyone moving.

As a group, the girls shuffled closer to the desk, then stopped. No one wanted to go to the other side, where Lady Stella usually sat so regally, her back straight, her expression calm and reassuring.

Adora almost changed her mind. What if she told everyone they should leave, not mess with Lady Stella's desk, and find another way to rescue their friends? She shook her head to clear it. No, they had to do this—now. "Maybe someone should open the drawer?" she said, still a little hesitant.

No one stepped forward.

Finally, Leona said, "For stars' sake, let's just get it over with!" She edged behind the desk and opened the drawer.

"Oh!" she gasped. Her golden glow paled, and her eyes widened in shock.

"What?" cried Adora. "What is it?"

She hurried to the other side, but Leona half closed the drawer and blocked her view.

"It's n-n-n-nothing," Leona stammered. "Everything is fine. I just saw a twelve-legged rainbow orb spider in there."

"Oh," said Gemma, looking interested. "Can I see?"

"No!" Leona said quickly. She peered back inside. "It's gone already." She smiled a little shakily. "You know me. I can't stand the sight of any creepy crawly." Then she reached into the drawer and pressed the button.

Behind them, the hidden door in the back wall slid open. Again, the girls exchanged glances. *This is it*, Adora thought. She set her Star-Zap on flashlight mode, and the others followed her lead. Then she started down the curving metal stairs, the line of Star Darlings behind her.

CHAPTER
6

"Wait!" Adora called up the stairs just as the last girl, Astra, was about to close the door behind them. "We need to keep the door open so we can get out when we're done."

"Okay," said Astra. "I'll do it."

Of course Adora trusted Astra. The Starling had, after all, recently come back from a successful mission. How difficult could it be to leave the door open just a crack? But Adora liked to control every experiment as best she could, and that went stardouble for times like those. She hurried back up the steps, waving the others forward.

Adora checked that the door was open, just a bit,

then turned to leave. But she heard a soft murmur. Voices drifted through the crack.

"Wait!" she whispered. "It's Lady Stella! And she's talking to someone."

Adora stood on the top step uncertainly. Should she and Astra catch up with the others? Or should they eavesdrop and maybe learn a thing or two about Lady Stella? She decided to listen in.

"Can you hear anything?" Adora whispered to Astra.

Astra cocked her head, concentrating. "Not really." She reached into her sports bag and took out two empty water bottles. She handed one to Adora. Then she placed the other one against the wall, the bottom against her ear.

"Don't laugh," she told Adora softly. "It transmits the sound and helps you hear. I caught my little brother eavesdropping on my parents this way!"

Adora lifted the bottle. She could hear a little more clearly, it was true, but it was still more mumbling than actual words.

Then the bottle slipped from her hands. It clattered to the solar metal steps. The voices stopped, and Adora froze. She and Astra stood as still as statues. Finally, the voices continued. Adora bent to pick up the bottle. Then a thought struck her: what if she had to sneeze?

All of a sudden, as if the mere thought of sneezing could make it happen, she felt a tingle in her nose. *For stars' sake*, she thought. *This is ridiculous.* She clamped two fingers on the sides of her nose as Astra looked at her curiously. Finally, the feeling passed.

"Are you all right?" Astra whispered. Adora nodded, gesturing that they should listen through the water bottles again. *More star craziness*, she thought.

But Lady Stella and her visitor must have moved closer to the back wall. Adora could hear them more clearly now.

"This is happening even faster than I imagined," Lady Stella was saying. "Starland is losing energy every starday."

The headmistress sounded the same as ever, calm and steady. If she thought the energy shortage was a serious problem, wouldn't she be anxious? And if she was engineering the whole thing, wouldn't she sound more pleased?

A second voice answered. "On my end, wish energy scientists have been working hard to . . ." Adora heard the rustle of clothing as the Starling moved farther from the door, her voice fading. Adora could just make out the words *Cosmic Transporters . . . swift trains . . . energy supplies . . . a true crisis.* Then the voice sounded a bit more clear: "Two schools have temporarily shut down. And more may follow. It may be time to tell them. You can't keep it secret any longer."

Tell who what? Adora wondered.

Lady Stella spoke next, but Adora couldn't catch anything at all. Astra grabbed Adora's arm. "I recognize that other voice!" she hissed.

"Who is it?"

"I'm not sure. I don't think I know her, really, or have heard her say more than a few words before. I have to hear more."

Astra paused. "Or maybe I could just . . ." She flicked a wrist so the door opened a tiny bit wider. Then both girls peered through the opening. They saw Lady Stella's back and a figure in a lavender cloak facing her. Astra leaned closer. Suddenly, the door whooshed shut.

"Odd," Adora heard Lady Stella say. "I thought that door was closed. . . . I must have left it open when I *mumble mumble*."

Did Lady Stella think she'd left the door open when she trapped Cassie, Tessa, and Scarlet? Or was she talking about something else entirely, like checking Wish Orbs?

It was so starmazingly confusing.

"Adora? Astra? We're waiting."

The Star Darlings were calling to them softly from the foot of the stairs. They couldn't waste any more time trying to listen. Adora squared her shoulders. They had to rescue their friends. And hopefully, when they did, Scarlet would know of another way out of the caves. Because now they were trapped, too.

The stairway to the caves wound round in spirals. At any given moment, Adora couldn't see past the step she stood on. Finally, she reached the bottom, pushed past the other Star Darlings, and once again led the way.

Plop . . . plop. The sound of dripping water grated on her nerves. Sage, behind her, stepped on her heel.

"Star apologies," Sage told her. "But maybe you could go a little faster?"

"Yes!" Gemma called down from behind them. "This is a rescue mission, you know!"

It was true that Adora didn't like to hurry. She walked the same way she thought: slowly and methodically. Haste, in the long run, interfered with reaching correct conclusions. Still, Adora moved a little more quickly. She wanted to help Tessa, Cassie, and Scarlet as much as anyone else did.

Finally, she reached a split in the cave. Now which

way should they go? Remembering other visits, she turned left. Slowly but almost surely, she led the girls down one long tunnel into the next. Really, it wasn't so bad down there. Even without Lady Stella's guidance, they were moving along.

Adora was congratulating herself on her leadership skills when she bumped smack into a boulder blocking the way. Could they squeeze past it?

She examined the passage more closely. Not even the thinnest Starling in Starland could get through. They'd have to take a detour.

Adora took the group to the right. She made a second right, then a third. By her calculations, that should have taken them around the boulder. Instead, they wound up in the same spot—directly behind it.

This time, they'd go left, Adora decided.

"You know," said Leona a few starmins later, when they found themselves stuck behind the boulder once more, "maybe this is some elaborate practical joke." She shot an angry look at Astra. "And no one likes a practical joker."

"What? Don't give me that solar flare, Leona. You know those jokes were out of my control. And do you think I'm having fun wandering around these tunnels? My star ball game must be over by now. Coach Geeta will bench me for a double starweek because I left in the middle. And I don't even know who won!"

Astra checked her Star-Zap to see if she could get the score, but the screen stayed dark. "*Starf!*" she said. "I forgot. Star-Zaps don't work underground."

"Except for the flashlights," Adora corrected Astra— accuracy was always important!—as she plowed ahead, mentally crossing off tunnel routes they'd already taken.

Then she stopped short. How could they possibly be behind the boulder again?

"If *we're* getting frustrated," Gemma said, hiccupping back a sob, "I can't even imagine what Tessa, Cassie, and Scarlet are going through. You know, Tessa likes wide open spaces. She's probably feeling claustrophobic."

Gasping, Gemma clutched her own throat. "I'm feeling it, too! I remember when Tessa and I were wee Starlings, and we got stuck in a Flash Vertical Mover. We didn't have any wish energy manipulation skills yet and—"

"*Starf!*" someone yelped.

"Sage?" Adora said, swiveling around. "Was that you?"

"Yes," Sage said with a groan. "I stubbed my toe."

Secretly, Adora was grateful that Sage's cry had at least ended Gemma's story. All the whining and bickering was distracting. And they really had to find the others.

"Piper!" she called, waving the Starling to her. "Can you sense if the girls are nearby?"

"Why, Adora!" Piper said, sounding surprised. Astra could hear the smile in her voice. "You're asking me to use my intuition? I'm flattered."

"Just do it," Adora said calmly. "I've used up all my reasoning skills, and you know I have an open mind. Besides, I think everyone has just about had it."

Piper closed her eyes and swayed dreamily. Adora tapped her foot impatiently. Finally, Piper opened her eyes. "I do sense another being."

"You do?"

All the girls leaned toward Piper eagerly. "She's coming closer. I believe we just need to wait." She paused, concentrating. "It might be Tessa or Cassie or Scarlet." She closed her eyes again. "Then again, it might be—"

"A bitbat," said Adora, stepping back as the small winged creature swooped in front of the girls.

The bitbat fluttered its wings, hovering in place. It held Adora's gaze for a moment. Then it went down the line of Star Darlings, stopping in front of each girl. Most stepped back, trying to put some distance between themselves and the creature. But Leona stared at it intently, actually edging closer.

"Leona!" said Adora. "What are you doing? You don't like bitbats, remember? You're always saying you're afraid they'll get caught in your hair."

Leona started to toss her curls, remembered herself, then pulled her hair back with both hands. "Of course I don't like them! But maybe this bitbat is the one that landed on Scarlet that time and it's trying to tell us something."

Leona looked at the bitbat again, then shook her head. "Forget it. That's crazy."

"Maybe; maybe not," said Adora. "The only way to find out is to give it a chance."

The bitbat flew to Adora, gave a funny little nod, then took off slowly down the tunnel back the way they'd come. Adora followed close behind, and the others filed after her.

The tunnel twisted again and again. Adora lost track of their path. *Stars crossed this works*, she thought.

At last the bitbat paused in front of a sheer stone wall.

"Well, this is just starmendous," Leona said crossly. "There's nothing here. What a waste of time."

Adora shook her head. "We don't know that yet. Cassie?" she called. "Tessa? Scarlet?" Her voice echoed eerily through the chamber.

The girls held their breath, waiting. But no one answered.

Adora sighed, disappointed. "Come on, bitbat," she urged. "Show us why you brought us here."

The bitbat swooped close to the wall, its wings brushing the stone. It moved around on the wall, almost in a pattern. . . .

"It's making a rectangle!" Adora exclaimed.

With every bitbat movement, the gray stone brightened, until Adora realized they were looking at a holo-screen.

The bitbat bowed, then flew away. They all stared at the screen, wondering what on Starland it could possibly mean.

"This is it," Piper said with certainty. "Tessa, Scarlet, and Cassie are on the other side of the wall. I can feel it. They just can't hear us."

Adora snapped her fingers at the holo-screen. She waved her hand in front of it. She placed her palm at different spots, hoping a hand scanner would appear. The screen stayed blank.

"Let's try our Power Crystals," Libby suggested.

"Yes, they were such a startacular success before," Leona said.

"Don't be sarcastic." Adora shook her head. "You never know."

Libby, Sage, Astra, and Vega waved their Power Crystals, but again, nothing changed.

Leona couldn't seem to help herself. "Like I said . . . big success."

Leona appeared to be correct. But Adora had a hypothesis and she wouldn't give up: if they activated the screen, they would find their friends. But how?

She searched again for a button, a lever, a scanner. They all set their Star-Zaps on the strongest flashlight mode, and she looked again, hoping to find something she'd missed. But there was nothing.

"Hey!" said Vega suddenly. "What about a password?"

"Great idea, Vega," said Adora. "Let's each try a word or phrase," she suggested. She knew it was a moonshot, but it was better than just standing there, doing nothing.

Piper stepped forward. "Dreaming is believing."

"Password denied," said a Bot-Bot voice as the phrase appeared on-screen, as well.

"Well, at least we know there is a password," Adora said reasonably.

Leona went next. "Wish Pendant," she practically hissed.

Nothing.

"We're never going to guess it!" Gemma cried. "It could be anything under the stars!"

Adora whirled around to calm Gemma, and her Star-Zap flew out of her hand and crashed to the floor. "Oh, moonberries!" she snapped, using her roommate's favorite new curse.

The holo-screen lit up. "Password accepted," said the voice, and a door slid open.

Inside, Cassie, Scarlet, and Tessa huddled on the ground.

Tessa jumped up, rushing to meet them. "Thank the stars you're here!" she cried. "Did you bring any food?"

Everyone talked at once, and it was impossible to make out what anyone was saying.

"Wait a starmin!" Adora held up a hand. "Let's settle down and find out exactly what happened. Cassie, since you sent the holo-letter, why don't you explain?"

Cassie gestured at the room, which was filled floor to ceiling with shelves of ancient holo-books. "Okay, but come inside. I have to show you something important."

"First things first," said Tessa, looking expectantly at her sister.

Gemma handed Tessa the container of ozziefruit, along with some wrapped astromuffins.

Tessa flung her arms around her sister. "Star salutations, Gemma! You're the best sister ever! I'll tell Mom I was the one who left the barn door open that time when all the galliopes ran off."

"Good," Gemma said. "Because it *was* you."

Adora and the rest of the Star Darlings joined Cassie and Scarlet inside the room. With twelve girls and hydrongs of books, it was a tight squeeze. Scarlet stood to the side, careful to keep her distance as best she could. But Cassie pulled her into the center of the group.

She quickly explained how Scarlet had found another entrance to the caves through a supply closet, and how her special bitbat had brought them to the room.

"Hey!" said Gemma. "That must have been the same one we saw!"

"Anyway," Cassie said, "we found this." She held out an ancient-looking holo-book with a five-point star pulsing on the deep purple cover. "It's hard to read. The writing is dim and in some old-fashioned style. But there's one part . . ."

Her voice trailed off as she flipped through the pages. "Here!" She stopped about halfway through, and a holo-picture rose in the air, showing twelve girls in a circle. Each Starling had her own Wish Blossom. Energy from the flowers was flowing into the circle's center, gathering in a ball of light.

"I can't see from back here," complained Leona. "What does it say?"

"The writing explains a prophecy," Cassie explained. "An ancient oracle that predicts the future." She pointed out some words as they hovered in the air. "This part tells about twelve Star-Charmed Starlings who have a special gift: the ability to grant wishes and gather powerful wish energy."

"Twelve?" Adora said slowly. "So that must be us. We're the Star-Charmed Starlings!"

Adora smiled at Scarlet. If she had to take sides in the Leona versus Scarlet battle of the roommates, she might just choose the serious loner over the social flutterfocus. Who else would have explored the tunnels and found that room?

Without thinking, the girls drew together in a circle. Even Scarlet reached out to hold hands with Sage and Clover. They looked at one another in awe and disbelief.

"There's more," said Cassie. "The oracle says we save Starland."

The rest of the Star Darlings gasped in unison.

"Save Starland? From what?" Clover asked.

"I don't know," said Cassie.

Adora stared. Could that be what Lady Stella had been talking about in her office?

It was all so unbelievable that Adora found it difficult to take in. A moonium thoughts flew through her mind, lightning fast.

Why us? she wondered. Adora admired, respected, and basically liked all the other Star Darlings. Really, they were starmazing. But for them to be chosen like that, above all others on Starland . . . it took her breath away. Sure, they had been selected to go down to Wishworld ahead of the rest of their classmates. That was special enough. But the thought that they were actually part of an ancient prophecy . . . and that they were supposed to save Starland . . . from something—that was overwhelming news, indeed. It was a privilege, of course, but a huge responsibility, too. They had the weight of the worlds on their shoulders.

Still, it was an opportunity to change the course of Starland. Adora had always hoped to make a difference, to improve the planet with science *and* fashion. But this was something much, much bigger.

"Talk about being in the starlight," Leona said. She shook her head in disbelief. "We're the twelve Star-Charmed Starlings."

The words sounded like Leona, but she spoke so quietly that Adora turned to study her for a moment. Ever since they'd started their rescue mission, Leona's glow had been pale. Something was definitely bothering her.

Adora gazed around the room to see how the others were taking the news. Sage and Libby were whispering excitedly, but everyone else seemed overwhelmed. Vega had a blank expression, as if this didn't fit into her practical worldview. Adora understood. Being selected to go on Wish Missions was one thing. But this took the Star Darlings to a whole other level—a cosmic one!

Finally, Cassie spoke again. "And this all brings us back to Lady Stella. She must know about this ancient oracle. She brought us together, after all. So why is she keeping this secret from us? Is it part of an evil plan?"

"It has to be!" Scarlet said loudly.

"Then why did she form the Star Darlings at all?" Sage countered.

"Well, if we're part of an ancient oracle, there's a good chance we would have come together on our own anyway," Cassie said seriously. "My theory is that Lady Stella organized us so she can keep an eye on us, control us . . . driving us apart on Starland with poison flowers and nail polish . . . interfering with our missions on Wishworld."

Scarlet took a deep breath and flung her hood over her head. "She could be keeping us from actually saving Starland," she said.

Adora weighed Scarlet's and Cassie's words. They made some sort of sense.

"I disagree!" cried Libby. "Lady Stella could just as easily be keeping everything secret to protect us. Too much knowledge could make us panic. It's a lot of pressure knowing the fate of Starland rests in our hands, isn't it?"

Adora nodded slowly, eyeing Gemma, who still held tightly to Tessa's hand.

"All that knowledge could have have jeopardized our missions," Sage added, "making us second-guess our every move—and put us in danger! Luckily we didn't know—"

"Ahem," said Clover. "Some of us haven't had a mission yet."

"Oops!" said Sage. "You know what I mean." She smiled broadly at Clover, then Gemma, then Adora. "You'll do starmendously, I know it! There's nothing to worry about at all."

"Yes, just the future of Starland," Scarlet added with a wicked grin. "No big deal, right?"

The girls erupted into arguments, some speaking in support of Lady Stella, some against. Adora listened to the debates, not judging, just thinking.

When there was a lull, Tessa stood up. "I really want to leave now. Can we all agree on that?"

"Yes, let's go back through the supply closet," Adora told everyone. "Lady Stella may still be in her office."

Everyone stood. But just as they turned to leave the room, the door slammed.

"Not again!" groaned Tessa. "Is it on a timer or is someone sabotaging us?"

The Star Darlings hurried to the door, pushing, pressing, waving Power Crystals, and flicking their wrists in a panic.

"Let's stay calm," Adora said quickly.

Cassie, next to her, turned paler than usual and whispered, "But we're all here. Who will rescue us now?"

"We'll have to find our own way out." Adora moved around the room, peering into all corners. "Maybe this is like Lady Stella's office, with a secret door."

"You know," Cassie said, joining her, "my uncle has written lots of detective novels. And in one of them, *The Trouble with Twilight*, there's a bookcase that spins around on a platform. The characters pull out a certain holo-book and it triggers the revolving bookcase, taking them into another room."

"Come on, Cassie," said Adora, shaking her head. "That's just fiction. The bookcase is a literary device to move the action along. We need to deal with real devices. Fact, not fiction."

Then a holo-title caught her eye: *The Great Escape.* Could it be? She pulled it off the shelf expectantly.

Cassie gasped.

"What?" Adora said a little impatiently. There was no revolving bookcase. Nothing even moved.

Silently, Cassie pointed to the empty space on the shelf—and the wall behind it. There was a hole in the wall, right at eye level, perfect for peeping.

Immediately, Adora peered through it. "Moons and stars!" she cried. "I see the Wish-House!"

She looked more closely. Yes, there it was: the tall windows, the glass roof, golden waterfalls of pure wish energy running down its sides.

Everyone rushed over, jostling a bit to get a better look. "There's got to be a way into the cavern," Adora said. She turned to Vega, who was good at figuring out the hedge maze. Maybe she could figure this out, too. "Any ideas?"

Vega rolled up her sleeves and moved random holo-books off the shelves. Nothing changed, but a satisfied expression crossed her face.

"Look!" she said. "There's a door around that peephole." Quickly, the Star Darlings pushed aside the remaining holo-books.

"A door!" said Tessa. "Do you think we can open it?"

"Not with your silly Power Crystals, I bet," said Leona. Then, before anyone could say or do anything else, she blinked at the wall. *Whoosh!* The door opened smoothly.

The girls wriggled over and under the shelves, making their way through the opening.

Adora was the last one through, and she joined the rest of the Star Darlings in the Wish-House, closing the door behind her. They stood there silently, staring. Lady Stella was already there, her back to them.

"Lady Stella!" Adora said with a gasp.

The headmistress whirled around. "Oh, my stars," she said, surprised. "I just sent you girls a holo-text saying a Wish Orb had been identified. When no one came to my office, I thought I'd check on the orb before you arrived. How in the stars did you get down so quickly?"

CHAPTER
8

How indeed? The Star Darlings all looked at each other, unsure of what to say. Adora took a deep breath.

"Well," she began, allowing herself to blush a shade of sky blue, "when we got your holo-text, it just so happened we were all together. You, um, must have left the door to your office open, so we let ourselves in. But you were nowhere to be seen. So star apologies, Lady Stella, but we used the secret drawer to open the passage. And here we are."

There wasn't one lie in the whole speech! Well, maybe some little light lies. *But still, not bad if I do say so myself,* Adora thought, relieved she'd managed to stick to a fuzzy kind of truth.

Lady Stella looked a bit doubtful and seemed about

to say more. But then the sunlight streaming into the cavern brightened dramatically—Adora had asked herself startime after startime how that worked underground—and Lady Stella bowed her head. "It must be time. Come, girls."

The Star Darlings moved to the center of the Wish Cavern and gathered around the grass-covered platform.

Adora's mind, usually so focused, buzzed with ideas, theories, and possibilities. That secret room . . . had someone tried to trap them there? Or was the door on a timer? And why was Lady Stella keeping so many secrets? Who had been that mysterious visitor in her office?

Adora's thoughts switched to the upcoming mission as the platform opened and a Wish Orb floated up into the room. The glittering ball could choose her, Adora knew. But she wouldn't get that special feeling so many of the others had at the sight of their orbs. She just didn't have that intuitive sense.

A couple of Wish Orb presentations before, in fact, she'd felt a definite tingle. *This is it*, she'd thought. *This Wish Orb is mine. I'm going on the mission!* But instead, the orb had settled right into Cassie's waiting hand.

Now she didn't have the slightest sense the orb would stop at her. It hovered between Gemma and Clover, and Adora sighed. She'd just have to wait until next—

Suddenly, the orb dipped and moved, swaying as if blown by a breeze. It first flew to Cassie, who unthinkingly reached out for it but then drew back her hand. Then it continued, moving a bit jerkily, to stop directly in front of Adora.

Adora held out her hands, and the orb landed on her palm as softly as a flutterfocus.

"The orb has chosen," Lady Stella said, just as always. Adora felt everyone's eyes on her, and she smiled. Each girl smiled back, even Scarlet, but Adora felt the tension in the room. They'd just learned the fate of Starland was in their hands—*and* they'd been trapped underground!

The gravity of the situation hit Adora like a load of starbricks. She'd be traveling mooniums of floozles away to a distant planet, away from her family and friends and everything she knew in the middle of a wish energy crisis. What if she got trapped there?

Adora brushed aside the thought. She would handle anything that came her way with logic and clarity, and it would turn out all right.

"That's it, then, girls," Lady Stella said with a sigh. She gathered herself and moved gracefully to Adora's side. The headmistress reached for Adora's hand and gave it a reassuring squeeze. Adora couldn't help herself:

she squeezed back. And for a moment, all doubts about Lady Stella flew out of her mind.

Aboveground once more, Adora hurried to get ready. She had to choose some Wishling clothes from her Wishworld Outfit Selector and compose a reminder list of everything she needed to do on Wishworld. Chronological order would be best, she thought—from folding up her shooting star to identifying her Wisher to collecting the wish energy.

Another list spelling out Wishworld tips would be helpful, too: keep track of the Countdown Clock, monitor energy levels, use the Mirror Mantra, figure out her special talent.

Adora walked into her dorm room, already starting to holo-type, her eyes on her Star-Zap. "Tessa?" she called. "Are you here?"

"We're all here," said Cassie.

Adora looked up with a start. The Star Darlings were grouped around the room, leaning toward her expectantly, as if they'd been waiting for her.

"What's going on?" she asked.

"Don't go!" said Leona, rushing over and flinging her arms around her tightly.

Adora waited a moment and then carefully removed herself from the embrace. She took a few steps back.

"Do you know how dangerous this mission could be?" Leona said, taking a few steps forward. "Someone is trying to stop us! Who knows what they will do?"

"Lady Stella *is* very powerful," Vega added.

"Anything could happen," Scarlet said.

"Stay home and bake astromuffins with me," Tessa cried.

All those Starlings in agreement! That was concerning. Clover wasn't telling any circus stories or cracking any jokes. And Cassie—smart as a glow-whip Cassie—was nodding seriously.

Adora looked at Sage and Libby, the strongest Lady Stella supporters. "What do you two think?"

They exchanged looks and Sage spoke up. "We want you to be safe. We don't want you to go, either."

Adora sat down at her lab table, her back to her friends. This was starmendously unusual. Everyone had come to her room to try to convince her to stay on Starland. Adora had read about this sort of gathering in a scientific holo-journal just the other starday. *Instarvention*, it was called.

In the holo-article, an astro-energy scientist on a quest to spot the mythical Galliope Comet could not stop looking through her telescope. She missed meals, bright days, even her own wedding. Finally, her family lifted her from her observation post, removed the telescope from her hands, and fed the scientist her favorite food—gamma-chip clusters—until she saw reason.

Reason, Adora said to herself. A key concept. Was it reasonable to go on the mission? Adora was nothing if not rational. She'd weigh the evidence.

First and foremost, no Starling had been hurt on Wishworld . . . at least, not yet. There had been Leona's return trip to Starland, during which she almost hadn't made it back . . . but that had been more of a cosmic fluke, Adora thought, since it hadn't happened again.

Plus, if she didn't go, Starland would definitely be in worse shape than it was now. There'd be no chance for extra wish energy. If she did go, she could very possibly help.

Besides, Adora felt confident she could reason her way out of any situation. As Lady Stella said, that was her strength: analyzing problems and figuring out solutions.

The good outweighs the bad, Adora decided. She turned to face the Star Darlings.

"I'm going," she announced. "And no one can convince me otherwise." She took a deep breath. "As one of the twelve Star-Charmed Starlings, it's my responsibility."

CHAPTER
9

The next morning, everything happened quickly. Right after breakfast, the Star Darlings headed to the Wishworld Surveillance Deck. Lady Cordial gave Adora the traditional Wishling backpack and keychain, and Lady Stella gave her last-minute instructions. *A cover-up?* Adora wondered. *Or a safety check?*

"Remember to figure out your special talent as quickly as possible," Lady Stella said. "That could make all the difference."

"I'll do my best," Adora agreed. Maybe that had been the problem with Leona's mission: she hadn't used her special talent. Adora put that at the top of her checklist.

Lady Stella smiled down at her. "Adora," she said

softly, "much rests on your mission. Rely on your strength: your ability to study situations with an objective mind, your aptitude to examine any circumstance from a distance. And remember to recite your Mirror Mantra when your energy is low: 'Use your logic. You are a star!' You will do fine and make us all proud."

Adora nodded. If Lady Stella's concern was just an act, she was an accomplished actress.

Next Adora made sure her Wish Pendant—a sky-blue watch with a star-shaped face—was securely fastened. Then the Star Wranglers strapped her to a shooting star and she took off, with barely a good-bye.

The journey through the universe was a bit bumpy, with plenty of time for the Star-Zap's outfit selector function to change her clothes. She'd chosen rolled-up denim shorts, a sky-blue sleeveless T-shirt, and sneakers designed with bright blue sequin circles.

Finally, she changed her appearance, reciting the lines "Star light, star bright, the first star I see tonight: I wish I may, I wish I might, have the wish I wish tonight."

"There," she said, gazing into her Star-Zap mirror, totally satisfied. She'd lost her shimmery glow, and her blue hair had turned a light brown. She looked washed-out and dull—perfect for Wishworld.

When she landed in a field of clover, no Wishlings were in sight. So she folded her star, placed it carefully in her backpack for the return trip, and gazed around.

It was peaceful and quiet. Just then, Adora had an idea. She stepped carefully around the field, looking for a four-leaf clover.

There! She spotted one! Quickly, she plucked it out of the ground. How lucky could one Starling get? And while she normally didn't believe in luck—perseverance and hard work paid off more in the end, she thought— she certainly wouldn't discount it now.

She'd learned in her Wishling Ways class that Wishlings used these clovers to make wishes—similar to those fluffy white flowers they blew on. So you never knew when one would come in handy. Besides, if she didn't use it, she could always give it to Clover for a souvenir.

She was still bending over close to the ground when she heard voices. She froze. All of a sudden, cool, confident Adora wasn't sure what to do. She'd just gotten back from helping Tessa on her mission. She'd navigated the route, found Tessa, and done her best to make a difference, all with ease.

But now she was the one responsible for success or

failure. It crossed her mind that she could be the first to complete a mission without another Star Darling helping out on Wishworld. That would be starmazing!

"This way, campers!" someone called.

Adora lowered herself to the ground so she was hidden in the long grass and clover. She peered across the field.

A straggly line of wee Wishling girls was following a bigger girl—not quite an adult, but older than Starling Academy students.

"Let's march, campers!" the girl called out. "Left, right. Left, right, left."

The little girls stomped their feet and did their best to follow the directions. But the line looked even worse than before.

"Jenny!" one said loudly. "Are we going straight to lunch?"

"You bet, campers!" Jenny sang out, not turning around. "Our nature hike is ending just in time."

Adora knew all about camp. For as long as she could remember, she'd gone to star camp over the Time of Lumiere break, during the warmest season on Starland. She fondly remembered making lightyards in stars and crafts and singing "Moonbaya" around the campfire.

Adora realized that school must be out and the Wishlings were enjoying their summer vacation.

The camp group disappeared into the distance. Adora decided to follow while she checked her Star-Zap for directions to her Wisher. *It must be someone at the camp*, she thought.

Sure enough, the directions told her to cross the field like the campers, then take a short trail through a wooded area. Adora stopped at the edge of the trees. A rustic complex spread out before her in a large open space.

There were playing fields off to one side. Games were winding up, it seemed, and many centered on nets.

There was that one called "basket of balls" that Astra had talked about. And another with a long net stretched across a rectangular court, where Wishlings hit a small green ball back and forth using smaller nets. Some shouted "Service!" before hitting the ball, as if they expected a Bot-Bot waiter to come and take their food orders.

It all seemed rather silly to Adora.

Adora looked at the other side. Large tents, built on solid wood platforms, ringed half the clearing. Beyond the trees she spotted a lake with a small sandy beach, floating docks, and canoes that looked too heavy to hover like the ones back home.

Large ramshackle buildings filled the center of the clearing. Each building had a sign in front: OFFICE. NURSE. MESS HALL.

Then she thought she must have misread one of the signs. She paused and read it again: "'Mess hall.'"

Adora knew Wishling homes didn't have self-cleaning capabilities. Maybe at camp they just threw all their garbage into that one building.

A stream of Wishlings was heading into the mess hall as she watched. No one carried trash.

Then she spied the group of wee Wishlings she'd seen earlier. They were hurrying inside. Could they possibly be eating lunch there? She made a mental note in her Cyber Journal: *There is a strong possibility that Wishling campers eat garbage.*

Adora edged closer to the mess hall. She looked through a window and was relieved to see Wishlings sitting at picnic tables, eating what appeared to be regular Wishling food—not scraps of paper or old torn socks.

She was just about to amend her observation when one girl called out, "Where's the bug juice?"

Adora shivered. She'd just stick to water there. And she'd keep the observation in the journal, just in case.

Just then, a man hurried past, talking into a device like a Star-Zap but much clunkier. "Uncle Hal to Chef Jeff! Uncle Hal to Chef Jeff! Come in, Chef!"

Adora heard a crackling sound, and an indistinct voice answered.

"Running late," the first man continued. "Do not start lunch without me. Repeat: do not start lunch. First-day protocol must be maintained: Uncle Hal announces camp rules and greets campers. Repeat: first-day protocol must be maintained."

Adora was fascinated by this Wishling male, not a type she'd seen before.

The man—Uncle Hal—wore a T-shirt with a picture of a big brown creature on it. The creature had four legs and what looked like a big empty coatrack attached to its head. Beneath the picture, there was writing: *Director, Moose Lake Camp.*

Uncle Hal wore a big floppy hat, too, along with baggy shorts and white socks that went up to his knees. His nose was covered with some sort of white cream.

Uncle Hal stopped short when he noticed Adora by the mess hall. "Young lady!" he called out. "Did you just arrive? I need to make sure our campers and staff are accounted for. That's my job and my privilege."

Adora waved at a group of girls about her age walking

past. One girl, with short curly hair, waved back and smiled.

"I'm with them," she said, not answering his question.

"Oh, you're a CIT," Hal said, flipping through pages on his clipboard.

"Hmmm. It seems like everyone checked in already. Odd. What is your name?"

Adora looked him in the eyes and said, "My name is Adora. I'm a CIT." (She almost giggled. What did that even mean?) "You don't see my name on your list. But it doesn't matter."

"Hmmm," the man said again. "Your name is Adora. You are a CIT. I don't see your name on my list but it doesn't matter." He sniffed the air and lowered the clipboard. "Welcome, Adora. Do you smell prune bran muffins?"

Adora had learned about lots of foods in her Wishers 101 class. But prune and bran? Those were new ones.

"Never mind," Uncle Hal continued. He grinned, and Adora couldn't help smiling back. He was goofy and a little self-important but nice. "You can call me Uncle Hal."

Without waiting for a reply, he went on. "Right now, it's time for lunch." He puffed out his chest a bit. "Of course they won't start without me."

Adora snuck a look at her Star-Zap, trying to figure out if her Wisher was inside the mess hall. No, her Wisher was—

"Adora!" Uncle Hal said sternly. "There are no cell phones at camp. You should know that."

"Oh! Of course!" Adora said quickly.

"You must bring it to the office. They'll hold it for you there. And you can pick up your camp T-shirt at the same time."

"Yes, I'll do that before lunch," Adora told him. She had no intention of letting the Star-Zap out of her sight for one starmin. It was too important a tool.

Uncle Hal nodded, then strode off to the mess hall. Idly, Adora wondered if he was indeed anyone's uncle.

Smiling, Adora walked away, checking her Star-Zap. It directed her to the waterfront. Quickly, Adora made a detour to pick up the shirt—marked with the words *Counselor in Training*.

So that's it, she thought. *CIT!*

After stuffing the shirt in her backpack, she hurried to the lake.

It was pretty there. The water was a soothing shade of blue. A circle of tall, leafy green trees provided shade. And the brightly colored canoes were lined up on the side of the beach. She walked closer, peering all around.

Where was her Wisher?

Adora looked down at her watch. It glowed slightly. She was getting close. She edged to the canoes. Her Wish Pendant brightened.

"Hello?" she called. "Anybody here?"

No one answered, but Adora thought she heard a noise.

She walked to a large silver canoe and squinted at a shadow between the seats.

It was a girl, sitting on the canoe's bottom and leaning back so she was almost lying down. She had big green eyes and straight brown hair that fell to her shoulders, and she wore a Moose Lake CIT T-shirt.

Yes! Adora's Wish Pendant glowed with a brilliant light. She'd found her Wisher!

CHAPTER
10

"Hello," Adora said.

The girl in the canoe turned away, as if she couldn't bear to face her. "Are you looking for me?" the girl asked quietly.

"Yes," said Adora, stepping into the canoe. It wobbled a bit, so she quickly sat down in the nearest seat at the other end. "I'm Adora."

The girl mumbled a response.

"What?" said Adora loudly.

The girl said even more quietly, "My name is *mumble mumble.*"

"Speak up!" Adora said a little brusquely. This was getting tiring. What was so difficult about saying your name?

The girl sat up, her fair skin turning a bright red. "My name is Hannah."

"Okay," said Adora. "So, Hannah. Do you want to get lunch?" Traveling through space had made Adora very hungry, and she thought she could feel out her Wisher as they ate.

Hannah shook her head.

"Why not?"

Hannah shrugged, then slunk back down to the bottom of the canoe.

Well, if this Wishling could wait to eat, so could Adora.

She considered the situation: what would be the fastest way to identify the wish? If she took care of everything quickly, she'd be back home in the blink of a star—*and* be the first Star Darling to grant a wish all on her own. That would be something.

Adora favored the direct approach. What if she just asked outright?

"Hannah, do you have a special wish?"

"Huh?" The girl was so startled that she spoke loud and clear.

"Do you have a special wish?" Adora repeated. She sat back, waiting patiently—except that she couldn't stop tapping her toe.

Hannah drew herself into a ball, her arms hugging her legs. She looked for all the worlds like a Starland pricklepine curling up for protection.

Adora sighed. This wasn't going well at all. "Clearly, you're a shy Wish—I mean, girl." She smiled widely, if a little falsely. "Some of my best friends are shy."

That was the truth. Adora considered Cassie a friend. Yes, Cassie was outspoken about her conspiracy theories, and she'd managed a Wishworld mission just fine. But she'd barely spoken to anyone her first double starweek at school. And she'd dreaded going on a mission until that poisonous nail polish had made her annoyingly braggy.

Maybe this girl was new at camp. Maybe she needed to be drawn out of her shell. That wasn't Adora's strength, but she'd give it a try.

"I'm new here," she told Hannah. "Is this your first time at camp, too?"

Hannah shook her head. "It's my fifth summer," she whispered.

Well, there went *that* idea. Suddenly, Adora had another idea. She reached into her backpack for the four-leaf clover. "Here," she said, handing it to Hannah.

Hannah's eyes widened. "A four-leaf clover. For good luck!"

"Go on," Adora urged. "Make a wish."

Hannah blushed, turning her back to Adora. "I-I-I . . ." she stuttered. Then she stopped.

Clearly, Hannah wanted to make a wish. She just didn't want to make it in front of Adora. "I'll step away," said Adora, pleased with herself for understanding the situation so well.

She climbed out of the canoe and walked to the edge of the lake, deliberately leaving her Star-Zap—set on record—on the canoe bottom.

She waited a bit, counting—"one Starland City, two Starland City"—until she reached a hydrong, then returned to Hannah.

"Oops!" she said. "I left my cell phone here. I'm not even supposed to have one! I'd better bring it to the office."

Adora moved out of Hannah's earshot, then played the recording: "I wish I had the confidence to make friends," Hannah said, her voice thin and quiet.

Wish identification accomplished! Adora allowed herself a starsec to savor her success.

If she could help grant the wish right then, she'd definitely have the record for fastest time. "Not that I'm competitive," she added to herself under her breath. She turned back to Hannah.

"So," she said brightly, "I really think we should go to the mess hall. There are some girls there who seem really nice. You seem nice, too. Maybe we can all be friends!"

Hannah stood up, rocking the canoe. "You were eavesdropping!"

Adora groaned. Now they were back in that fuzzy area of truth versus lies. Was it okay telling a little light lie to grant a wish? In all fairness, that was a technicality. Strictly speaking, Adora had heard the *recording*, not Hannah as she was making the wish.

"Star—I mean, I'm sorry, Hannah," Adora said. "It was none of my business." (That actually was a lie. Hannah's wish was most certainly her business.)

Hannah sank onto a canoe seat. "It's all right, I guess. You're new here. You'd like to make friends. I understand. But you see, I did have friends here. Two best friends. We started camp together the first year we were old enough for sleepaway. We were close right from the start. Uncle Hal called us the triplets. Every summer was fun. And we kept in touch during the school year, too."

Hannah's voice caught, and she paused. She squeezed her eyes shut, holding back tears.

Adora nodded encouragingly. But she couldn't resist a look at the Countdown Clock on her Star-Zap. She was definitely on track for breaking the wish-granting record.

"But this year, my friends didn't come back," Hannah continued. "One is traveling with her family. The other decided to go to science camp instead."

Science camp? Really? Why couldn't that girl have been my Wisher? Adora wondered. It would have been a much better match. This Wishling was a wreck!

"And my parents didn't tell me any of this until the day before camp started," Hannah whimpered. "So I had to come! And now I'm here alone."

Finally, tears slipped down her cheeks.

"Well, you're not really alone," Adora said logically. "You're surrounded by girls your age and other people. Were those other CITs here other summers, too?"

"Some," Hannah admitted.

"And do you like them?" Adora prodded her.

Hannah shrugged. "I guess so," she said.

"So just go up to them and talk. They're in the mess hall right now!" *There*, she thought. *Problem solved. Wish granted.*

"It's not that simple," said Hannah.

"It can be," Adora insisted. "You're talking to me, right?" Then she added quickly, in case Hannah thought that she could be her new friend, "You should know I'm only a . . . a TCIT—a Temporary Counselor in Training. I'll be leaving very soon."

"I didn't know that was allowed," said Hannah eagerly. "Maybe I can be a TCIT, too, and leave with you?"

This isn't working at all, Adora thought exasperatedly. "Uncle Hal said he'd make an exception for me, just this once. It turns out I have a family emergency. Something really bad happened. To my house. And we have to . . . to move and . . . and . . . other stuff!"

Adora stopped, realizing she'd just told outright lies. She'd expected to tell some. After all, she couldn't be on a strange planet and fit in without lying. But she hadn't thought they would be such big fat ones.

"Oh!" Hannah cried harder. "You're going through something terrible. And here I am, so worried about myself and my problems! I feel horrible."

This was even worse. Awkwardly, Adora put her arms around the Wishling. "There, there," she said. "Don't cry."

Hannah sobbed.

Adora raised her voice and said, "Don't feel bad on my account. Really." These lies were definitely backfiring! "I have another idea for how you can make friends. And it will make me feel better if you feel better."

"Okay." Hannah wiped her eyes.

"Do all the CITs share a tent?"

"Yes."

"So it will be like a sleepover every night!" Adora exclaimed. "You'll definitely make friends. You know, whispering in the dark, sharing secrets." Adora didn't know much about sleepovers, actually. But that's what happened when Libby had one right before Piper's mission.

"I chose the bed in the corner, away from everyone else. I'm too far to whisper. So that's not going to happen." Hannah sniffled.

"What about your CIT job? Won't you be working with other girls?"

"No, I'm helping with arts and crafts. Uncle Hal is in charge, and I'll be his assistant. That's why I'm just hanging around today. There aren't any special activities until tomorrow." She sniffled louder.

Oh, starf! Was Hannah going to burst into tears again? Why was this Wishling so emotional? They were such an unlikely match!

"You should just leave," said Hannah, sensing Adora's annoyance. "Go on. You can hang out with the other CITs." She reached to the ground, tracing a sad face in the sand.

Adora frowned. Now Hannah didn't even want to talk to her. She'd rather draw starmojis in the sand.

Just then, Adora heard a strange buzzing. From the corner of her eye, she spied a tiny winged creature flying around her head. Peering closer, she saw it had a yellow-and-black-striped body and looked a bit fuzzy—like a glitterbee without the sparkle.

Two more Wishworld insects flew down from some sort of nest in a nearby tree. They joined the first, and then even more swarmed closer. *Bzzzz. Bzzzz.*

Adora held out a finger, hoping one would land on her so she could observe it more closely.

"What are you doing?" Hannah jumped out of the canoe. Her voice rose in panic.

What was with that Wishling? One starmin you could barely hear her speak; the next she was practically shrieking. It was like Hannah was on an emotional star coaster.

"Obviously, I want to get a closer look," Adora said, trying not to snap. It would be an interesting observation to add to her journal.

"Those are bees! You're going to get stung!"

Stung? Glitterbees were sweet and gentle. On Starland, no insects or bugs had stingers, and it took a moment for Adora to realize what that meant. She sat very still and considered the situation. Should she stay close to the bees as an experiment? What would a Wishworld bee sting feel like? Would it be worth it to be able to make an accurate observation?

In the end, Adora decided against it. And that was just as well, since the bees were flying over to Hannah, attracted to her movements.

The bees circled Hannah as she moved left and right, trying to dodge each one. Some landed on her arms and legs. One landed on her nose.

"Ouch! Ouch! They're stinging me!" she cried, batting them away.

Adora started running toward the dock. "Follow me!" she cried. Hannah followed close behind her. "Now jump in!" Adora commanded. Hannah hesitated for a split second, grabbed her nose, and leaped.

A moment later, she popped to the surface. "That was really smart," she told Adora as she paddled to the shore. She shook herself. "I just wish I had taken my sneakers off first."

"You did what you had to do," said Adora. "I'm glad it worked."

Hannah held out her arms. "Look at all those bee stings," she said. "They really hurt."

Adora examined the red bumps individually. Curious, she touched the one on the end of Hannah's nose. Hannah flinched.

Adora watched the bump get smaller . . . and smaller . . . and smaller . . . until it disappeared.

"Hey, my nose doesn't hurt anymore!" said Hannah.

Adora touched another sting, on Hannah's arm. That one disappeared, too.

"That's crazy!" said Hannah, holding out her other arm to show Adora more stings.

Adora touched the red spots one by one. They all disappeared.

"Wow!" Hannah said. "How did you do that?"

Thinking quickly, Adora spotted a bottle on a nearby picnic bench and picked it up. The label read SPOT-ON SUNSCREEN. Adora had no idea what sunscreen even was. But when she opened it, it looked like the cream Uncle Hal had been wearing on his nose. She figured it wouldn't hurt Hannah. And it wouldn't hurt to tell just one more little light lie.

Adora ran one finger along the bottle's cap. "I just put this on the bites!"

Hannah looked confused but shrugged. "I guess sunscreen helps bee stings, too."

Adora grinned. She'd just discovered her special talent: she could heal bee stings!

Then she noticed a scratch on Hannah's arm. "Can I try to make this better, too?" she asked.

Hannah nodded. So Adora smeared a bit of lotion on her arm, carefully touching the scrape, and like magic, that disappeared, as well.

She could heal scrapes and scratches and who knew what else!

But she had to get back to the matter at hand. "I'm glad I could help you," she told Hannah honestly. "That's why I'm here."

Hannah looked at her doubtfully. "There's no sunscreen that can fix friendships." She looked like she was about to cry again.

This wasn't going to be easy.

CHAPTER
11

A short while later, Adora was standing in the bathroom, which was a small building by the CIT tent. She gazed at her plain reflection in the mirror. Already she felt tired. Her energy levels must be getting low—and so soon into the mission! Dealing with Hannah and her emotions certainly took a lot of strength.

Adora had told Hannah she needed to "freshen up" before lunch. But really, she'd just wanted to refresh using her Mirror Mantra.

She leaned in close to the mirror and recited her lines: "Use your logic. You are a star!"

Immediately, Adora saw her reflection shift to her shimmery Starland self, all sparkle and glow. Adora grinned. She did indeed feel refreshed. Satisfied, she stepped away from the mirror and called, "Hannah!"

Of course her Wisher was too nervous to go to the mess hall on her own. She was waiting for Adora outside. But Adora wanted to say her Mirror Mantra again, this time away from the mirror, with her Wisher. That would definitely give them both strength.

"Coming," said Hannah in a small voice, knocking tentatively before she walked in.

Really, how timid could one Wishling be?

Slowly, Hannah walked inside, looking shyly at the floor.

"Come on, Hannah," said Adora. "Look at me so we can talk!"

Hannah lifted her downcast eyes. "Oh!" she gasped, falling back against the door.

Adora frowned. What was her problem now?

"Y-y-you're all sparkly!" Hannah stammered. "And your hair: it's blue!"

"What?" That couldn't possibly be true. Adora's heart thudded in her chest. Even in her shock, Adora took note of her rapid pulse. It was certainly an unusual state for her and worth reflecting on. "You're serious?"

Hannah nodded.

Slowly, Adora turned to face the mirror. It was true!

Her skin still shimmered, and her blue hair actually sent sparks flying into the air, a reaction to her heightened sense of danger. She recalled being taught that a Wishling should never see your true appearance. This was bad—very bad.

"Who—what—are you?" Hannah whispered.

Adora made a split-second decision. She would tell Hannah everything. But first: privacy. Like a science experiment gone haywire, this situation needed to be contained as quickly as possible.

She rushed to lock the door. It took her a moment to figure out the mechanism. When she whirled around, she saw a panicked Hannah slipping into the bathroom stall farthest away. Hannah closed the stall door with a click.

"You locked me in!" Hannah cried. "What do you want with me? Wait! Don't answer. Just don't come any closer! I have . . . I have . . ." Adora heard her rummaging around. "A toilet plunger! And I'm not afraid to use it!"

Adora took a deep breath. Then she knocked softly on the stall door.

"Hannah? Open up the door so we can talk. I may look different. But I'm still Adora. I won't hurt you."

"How do I know that? I need proof."

Adora could understand that. "Tell you what. I'll

unlock the outside door. Then I'll go in another stall, in case anyone comes in. You can leave whenever you like."

"Okay," Hannah said softly.

Quickly, Adora unlocked the door and sat down in another stall. *This is just too weird*, she thought, sitting on the uncomfortably hard seat. Why couldn't Wishlings come up with technology to make objects conform to individual bodies and preferences? And now she had to explain to her Wisher why she was glowing. What had gone wrong? None of her Star Darlings classes had ever covered a situation like that one!

Adora heard Hannah's door open. She half expected the girl to rush outside. Instead, the Wishling moved closer and stood outside Adora's door. "Go on," Hannah said.

Hannah hadn't run away. That was good. Now to explain. There was only one logical way to proceed: she had to tell the truth. "I'm from Starland," Adora began. She talked about her world, about Starling Academy and the Star Darlings and the energy crisis.

When she paused for a moment, Hannah said she could open the door.

Adora went on to explain what her mission was and how she had traveled to Earth. When she took a breath, Hannah said she could come out.

Hannah's eyes were wide. "It sounds unbelievable," she said, "but something is telling me that you're not making this up." She laughed. "Maybe it's your sparkly skin and your glittery blue hair that convinced me!"

The two girls leaned against the sinks as Adora finished her explanation. "So I discovered my special healing talent. That wasn't, ah . . . sunscreen. It was just me. What is sunscreen, anyway?"

"It's lotion that protects your skin from harmful sun rays," Hannah told her. Adora looked at her in shock. Imagine needing protection from a light source!

"Anyway," Adora concluded, "I know that you're my Wisher. So I need to help make your wish come true."

"Starland . . . Wishworld . . . granting wishes." Hannah shook her head in wonder. "I would like to help. Do you think if I just say, 'Okay, I'm good at making friends now,' you can get the wish energy and leave?"

"I don't think so," Adora said doubtfully. "It probably needs to be a genuine wish-come-true." She shrugged. "But let's try it anyway."

She held out her arm, bringing her Wish Pendant watch closer to Hannah. She smiled as the Wishling proclaimed loudly, "I feel so confident! I realize now how easy it is to make friends!"

But no rainbow of colors whooshed from Hannah

to the watch. She didn't give off one tiny spark.

"That was nice of you to try," Adora said. "But it's useless."

With those words, her heart beat faster once again. She didn't like those feelings. She was nervous. Upset. Clueless. She didn't have the starriest idea how to fix the situation.

What had she done to make things go horribly wrong? How would she ever be able to grant a wish when she couldn't even leave the bathroom?

Suddenly, the door to outside swung open. Hannah quickly but gently pushed Adora back into the stall. Adora hastily locked the door, then pulled up her feet when she realized even her sneakers were sparkling.

She heard footsteps. Someone said, "Hi, Hannah. I haven't seen you yet! How have you been?"

Hannah mumbled a soft, awkward response.

Adora opened the door very slightly, peeked out, and saw the girl who had waved earlier. She was so friendly. Why couldn't Hannah see that? It would make everything so much easier!

The girl finished quickly and left the bathroom without saying another word.

"Now what?" said Hannah in a normal-sounding voice when Adora came out again.

"I really don't know," said Adora. For the first time ever, she had no next step, no hypothesis to test.

"Well," Hannah said, "you need a hiding spot. You can't stay in this bathroom forever."

"I do have a tent," Adora said, wondering why she hadn't thought of it earlier. Why, oh why, wasn't she thinking straight?

"Great!" said Hannah. "You can set it up in the woods."

"Well, it is kind of big," Adora explained, "but it won't need to be hidden. It's invisible to Wishlings." She thought for a moment. "But I guess it shouldn't be too close so nobody will bump into it!"

"You can put it behind the CIT tent!" said Hannah.

Adora could, in fact, leave the bathroom. So why was her heart still racing? And why was her mind still a muddle?

The whole mission was more difficult than she could have imagined. Forget about finishing in record time—what if she never finished her mission at all?

A lump formed in Adora's throat. She couldn't swallow. She thought back to the previous day, when she'd suspected she was getting sick. If it really was star pox, she'd be in deep trouble. Who would take care of her on Wishworld?

Then one tear rolled down her cheek. *Oh!* Adora realized with a start: She wasn't sick. She was crying. It had been so long she'd almost forgotten what it felt like.

Hannah stared at Adora's pale blue tear. "It's like liquid glitter," she marveled. Then she patted Adora's arm. "It's okay. Just wait here."

Hannah brought back a long terry cloth robe. Adora slipped it on, the bottom sweeping the floor. She pulled up the hood so it covered her head and face.

"Lead the way," said Adora. "And fast."

The girls hurried outside, not pausing for a moment— not even when Uncle Hal called out, "Hannah! Why weren't you at lunch?"

"Not hungry!" Hannah squeaked out.

A distance behind the CIT tent, Adora opened her backpack and took out her folded-up tent. Immediately, it popped up to its full size.

"When are you going to pitch the tent?" Hannah asked.

For a moment, Adora was too confused to answer. Pitch a tent? Was that some kind of Wishling sport?

"The tent is right here, set up and everything," Adora said. "Remember you can't see it?"

"Can I go inside?" asked Hannah.

Again, Adora didn't know. They were really in uncharted waters. What if she wasn't allowed into the tent? What if Hannah could go inside but was still visible to Wishlings? Either way, they'd never get anything done.

"I'll try to lead you inside," Adora finally told Hannah. She opened the flap, took Hannah's arm, and steered her through the opening.

Inside, Hannah opened her eyes wide.

Well, at least she can see the interior, Adora thought. And it was impressive, if she did say so herself.

The star-shaped room was large and plush. Thick blue carpeting covered the ground from one end to the other. In the very center stood a huge bed, covered with fluffy pillows, all tinted a lovely shade of sky blue. Adora took off her backpack and dropped it to the floor.

Hannah stood for a moment with her mouth open. "This is unbelievable!" she said.

"Remember, you can't tell anyone about this!" Adora said warningly.

"Who would I tell, anyway?" Hannah replied. "Remember? I don't have any friends."

Adora felt sad for her.

Hannah walked around the perimeter, examining

the paintings of Starland that hung in every point. Looking at the pictures, Adora felt an unexpected pang in her stomach. That time she knew she was sick—homesick.

"This is amazing!" said Hannah. "But am I invisible, too?"

"I don't know!" Adora said. She peered outside. The girl from the bathroom and her friend were leaving the CIT tent and moving closer. "But we're about to find out."

"Uh-oh, that's Jess and Allie." Hannah quickly sat on the floor, putting her head in her hands, as if she was upset.

"I'm striking a pose," she whispered. "If they see me sitting in the middle of nowhere all alone, they won't even think it's strange."

The two girls walked past as if Hannah and Adora and the tent weren't there at all.

Adora and Hannah collapsed in a fit of giggles.

"We figured that out," Hannah said, catching her breath. "Maybe we can figure everything else out, too."

"Star salutations, Hannah," Adora said, still smiling. "That means 'thank you.'"

Hannah had snuck into the mess hall and returned with sandwiches, fruit, and cookies. She'd even brought Adora bug juice, which Adora learned wasn't made from bugs after all. In fact, it tasted a lot like starberry juice.

Now it was dark outside the cozy tent, and the girls were still trying to come up with a plan.

"I have to go to the CIT bonfire," Hannah told Adora. "But I'll come back later to make sure you're all right."

Adora sighed. Somehow it seemed she and her Wisher had switched places. She was supposed to make Hannah feel better, not the other way around.

Still, she appreciated everything Hannah was doing for her. And while her Wisher was at the bonfire, Adora would go back to her logical way of thinking. She would come up with a foolproof plan for Hannah to gain the confidence she needed to make friends.

Of course, the plan couldn't take Adora outside . . . so maybe she had better figure out how to fix her appearance first.

Oh, moonberries. Her mind was in a muddle once again. What should she try to take care of right then? And how would she accomplish any of it?

Adora leaned back on her pillows and stared at the

tent ceiling, waiting for inspiration. She yawned loudly. It had been quite a starday. She was starmazingly tired.

Across the tent, a lone mirror hung between a holo-photo of the Crystal Mountains and an artist's rendering of a florafierce field. All she had to do was walk across the floor, gaze at her reflection, and say her Mirror Mantra. That would definitely make her feel better. She really needed energy! But then she realized that she needed that strength just to reach the mirror.

Slowly her eyes began to close. She'd just rest for a few starmins. . . .

CHAPTER
12

"Adora, wake up!"

The next thing Adora knew, someone was shaking her shoulders and bouncing up and down on her bed.

She sat up quickly. "Cassie!" she exclaimed. "Am I late for Astral Accounting?"

Wait! Cassie wasn't even in her Astral Accounting class. And how had she gotten into her room, anyway?

Then it all came back in a rush: Adora wasn't in the Big Dipper Dorm. She was in a tent on Wishworld, and her mission was going starmendously wrong.

She'd been hoping she could handle it all on her own, but there was her helper Starling. Adora would not be the first Star Darling to complete a mission on her own after all.

Adora was pleased to see Cassie but a little put out at the same time. "I haven't even been here one day," she said with an edge to her voice. She glanced at her Star-Zap, which was sitting on a nightstand. "My Countdown Clock says I have lots of time left. You could have waited a little longer."

Cassie smiled at her gently. "Your energy levels were so low everyone was alarmed. Besides, look at you! You're shimmering and glittery and everything a Wishling is not. Something is really wrong. That must be draining your energy. You definitely need some help. That's why I'm here, Adora. Not to make you feel bad."

Adora slumped back against her pillows. Cassie was right. It actually felt good to have her close by, frowning in sympathy. Adora gazed at her friend: no sparkles, no glitter. Wishworld plain as could be. Adora would never have believed she'd ever be envious of dull skin and hair. But she was!

"Star salutations, Cassie," she said.

Cassie reached out for her hand. "How did it happen?" she asked. "How did you change back?"

"I don't even know," said Adora miserably. "I was in the bathroom, saying my Mirror Mantra. One starmin I had no sparkle; the next I was as shiny as a newborn Starling."

Again, a tear rolled down Adora's cheek. *This is ridiculous!* Adora thought. *I'm an emotional swift-train wreck.*

"You poor thing," Cassie said. She hugged her close for a moment, then looked at her thoughtfully. "We'll figure it out."

"Oh, Cassie!" Adora burst out crying. "Don't mind me. I'm just so glad you're here." *If sweet, sympathetic Cassie had taken on this mission,* Adora thought, *she'd have gotten Hannah to open up on her own, without resorting to trickery with a recording device!* She had a sudden thought. "Cassie, what was your Wish Mission?"

"To help a Wishling who wanted her teacher to appreciate her," Cassie replied.

"So you and your Wisher were a good fit?" Adora asked.

Cassie thought for a starmin, her brow furrowed. "Now that you mention it, I don't think we were! Or at least, we wouldn't have been. She was a real class clown. It only worked out because I was so"—she blushed Wishling pink—"um, braggy at the time."

Adora grabbed Cassie's hands. "Cassie, I think that our Wish Missions were mixed up!"

"Really?" said Cassie.

"Yes," replied Adora. "My Wisher is very sensitive. I almost don't understand her."

"Well, it makes sense, I guess," said Cassie. "Something seems to go wrong on every mission."

Adora pointed to her sparkly self. "And on this mission, more than one thing!"

"Well, maybe we can reverse your appearance," Cassie said.

Adora leaned forward eagerly. "Maybe we can!" She got out of bed, gave a small yawn, and began to move more quickly. "Let's re-create the scene. I was standing in front of the mirror, wearing my backpack." She grabbed her backpack and threw it over her shoulder, the key chain swinging.

"Then I said my Mirror Mantra."

Adora gazed deeply at her reflection and said, "Use your logic. You are a star!"

Immediately, Adora felt wide awake. But there was no appearance change. If anything, her glow grew stronger.

"That's okay," she told Cassie. "Trial and error. Scientists live by it."

"What if you said it backward?" Cassie suggested.

"Good idea!" Adora paused a moment, composing the mantra in her head, then said, "Star a are you. Logic your use."

Nothing.

Then she tried another approach. Instead of looking

in the mirror, she turned her back to it and said the mantra again. But Adora could tell by Cassie's expression that that hadn't worked, either. Neither did saying it backward while facing backward.

"Maybe we should go back to the bathroom," Adora said.

"I don't think we should take a chance that anyone sees you," Cassie said. "We can try a few more things first. I know the Power Crystals didn't make a difference on Starland, but on Wishworld, Astra's really did open a door. Say your Mirror Mantra, Adora, and I'll wave my crystal."

Cassie held out her lunalite, a cluster of teardrop-shaped jewels glowing with pink moonlight.

This has to work! thought Adora. She closed her eyes and said her Mirror Mantra one more time while Cassie waved the crystal all around her. Then she held her breath, expecting to feel the change from the tips of her glittery toes to the top of her sky-blue head.

Nothing!

Just then, Hannah walked into the tent. She and Cassie gasped at the same time. "Who is that?" they both cried.

"It's okay, Cassie. It's my Wisher. I told her everything," said Adora. Then she turned to Hannah. "This is my friend Cassie," she explained. "She's a Star Darling who's here to help." She filled Hannah in on what they'd been trying to do to reverse her appearance.

"Hmmm." Hannah thought a moment. "What did you do to look human?"

"I recited the 'Star Light, Star Bright' poem," Adora said. She grinned. "Good thinking, Hannah! Let's try that."

Adora recited the poem, but there was no change. "Should I say it backward?" she asked Cassie.

"Let's try the Power Crystal again while you say it the regular way first," said Cassie.

That time it worked! Once again, Adora looked like a Wishling—no glow, no sparks.

Quickly, she hugged Cassie, then Hannah. "You are the best Wishling ever!" she cried.

"Well, you're the best Starling," Hannah replied. She smiled at Cassie. "No offense."

Once again, Adora and Hannah burst into giggles. "I don't know why I'm laughing like this!" Adora said, clucking like a glow-hen and snorting. She had never been much of a giggler before she'd met Hannah.

Hannah pushed Adora so she faced the mirror and could see her own laughing expression. "Has anyone ever told you you're *Adora*-ble?" she asked.

Adora laughed so hard her sides ached.

"Okay, okay," Cassie finally said. "Your appearance is fixed. Now we can concentrate on the wish."

Immediately, Adora sobered.

"If you don't mind my asking, what is it?" Cassie said.

Adora and Hannah exchanged looks. "You tell her," said Adora. "It's your wish."

Hannah nodded. "I wish I had the confidence to make new friends."

Cassie gazed searchingly from Adora to Hannah. "You mean you don't want to be afraid to talk? You want to feel secure enough to be friendly and open? So you can make friends with people you don't really know?"

Hannah sighed. "That's it exactly. How did you know?"

"Because I know exactly how you feel." Again, Cassie glanced from Adora to Hannah. "And I have great news for you!"

Adora knew Cassie had had a hard time when she first got to Starling Academy. An orphan without siblings, Cassie had traveled often with her uncle, a best-selling novelist, and had a private tutor. So when she'd arrived at Starling Academy, she hadn't felt comfortable with other students—at first. *Hannah and Cassie really have a lot in common*, Adora thought. But right then, she just wanted Cassie to get to the point.

"So?" she prodded.

"Adora, you've already helped grant Hannah's wish. It's just that neither of you realize it."

Adora gripped Hannah's hand. "What is Cassie talking about? Did you make friends at the bonfire? You've been spending so much time with me, how did you even manage it?"

Hannah's eyes opened wide. "I didn't make friends at the bonfire. I made a friend right here."

Cassie grinned. "You bet your stars you have! Adora, you granted Hannah's wish by opening up to her and needing *her* friendship. You gave Hannah confidence. And just look at you two!"

She pointed down, and the girls noticed they were still holding hands. "You've bonded. You're real friends."

"Oh, my stars," said Adora, finally realizing it for herself. "We do have fun together."

Hannah giggled. "We are real friends," she agreed. "So what happens now?"

"Now your wish energy is supposed to fly through the air in a colorful stream, straight into my Wish Pendant."

Everyone looked at the watch expectantly.

When nothing happened, Adora rubbed her hands together, pacing back and forth. "Maybe you're not entirely there yet," she finally said to Hannah. "You need proof you're a friend worth having."

Hannah groaned. "So now I have to knowingly make a friend?"

Adora grinned. "Yup! But let's wait until morning. It's so late now everyone must be sleeping. You'd only make enemies if you tried now!"

That night, Adora stayed up for hours, thinking things through. If everything worked out, she'd be back on Starland before too long. And she still didn't know what to think about Lady Stella.

By the time the sun rose the next morning, she wasn't any closer to a conclusion. So finally, she closed her eyes.

She and Cassie slept through breakfast and well into the day while Hannah worked at the arts and crafts cabin. Right before lunch, the Starlings met her at the agreed-upon spot: a picnic table outside the mess hall.

Adora was so certain Hannah's wish would be granted that she'd packed up her tent and all her belongings.

"Okay," she said, getting right down to business. "Here come Jess and Allie. Call them over."

"Right now?" said Hannah. "Can't we have lunch first?"

"Now," Adora said firmly.

Hannah ducked her head, leaning down to scratch her knee. *A nervous gesture*, Adora thought, and her heart went out to her. This was difficult for Hannah. Just because Adora could march right up to the girls and start talking didn't mean it was easy for someone else.

"Do it fast," she advised. "It will be easier that way." She glanced at the girls. "And they seem to be in a hurry."

"Hey! Allie! Jess!" Hannah called loudly.

The girls stopped and looked at her in surprise.

Hannah sidled closer. "Um . . . what's going on?" she said much more softly.

"We have to see the nurse." Allie's voice sounded strained. "Look!" She and Jess held out their arms. Red blistery rashes streaked their skin. Jess scratched hers, making it look even worse.

"It's so itchy," Jess complained. "It's got to be poison ivy."

She glanced at Adora and Cassie curiously. "Oh," said Hannah, "Adora and Cassie are visiting for the day." She smiled. "They're my friends."

Jess nodded absently. "Well, that's nice. But we've really got to run. We must have gotten poison ivy at the bonfire. We woke up with the rash this morning, and we should get it taken care of as soon as possible."

The girls started to edge away.

Adora looked around, hoping for an idea, a way to get them to stay, and she noticed Hannah's knees. They were red and blotchy, too. "You have that poison ivy thing, too," she whispered loudly. "Tell them!"

"Oh!" said Hannah, raising her voice even louder than before. "I have it, too! On my knees!"

Everyone bent closer to look. "You're right!" said Allie. "Isn't it awful?"

"It is," Hannah agreed. "But you know, Adora has some amazing lotion for rashes and bug bites." She winked at Adora. "Maybe it would work on poison ivy, too."

The sunscreen! Hannah wanted her to pretend to use it so she could heal the rash—and maybe help the girls bond even more. Luckily, Adora had the bottle in her backpack. She'd been planning to examine its chemical makeup back on Starland. There wasn't much left. She hated to use it. But it had to be done.

She rifled through her backpack, feeling around for the bottle, pushing aside the tent, the camp T-shirt, and other Wishworld specimens she'd picked up. "Here it is!" she said triumphantly.

She poured out just a smidgeon.

"Is that enough?" asked Jess anxiously.

"Enough for all of you!" Adora said cheerfully.

She crouched down and applied the lotion to Hannah's knees first, then to Allie's and Jess's poison ivy patches. She made sure to hold her hand over each spot.

Starsecs later, all three girls were smiling. "Thank you!" Allie said. "That is amazing stuff!"

"I know, right?" said Hannah. "By the way, be careful by the canoes. There must be a beehive nearby. I got stung there yesterday."

"You did?" said Allie. "I am totally afraid of bees."

Adora and Cassie stepped away as the three Wishlings compared their camp histories of bites, stings, and rashes. Then they moved on to camp plays, swim tests, and Color War.

Color War? Adora didn't remember that one from Wishling History class. Hopefully, the war was pretend, since this was just camp, after all.

Then Hannah turned to Adora and smiled so widely that Adora knew her Wisher's wish had come true. Right on cue, wish energy streaked through the air, streaming into her Wish Pendant. Adora and Cassie watched, openmouthed. It was startastically beautiful.

"Let's all go to lunch together!" Hannah said, waving at the Starlings to join the group.

"Great!" said Allie.

"Hannah, I need to talk to you for a minute," said Adora.

"We'll save seats, Hannah," Jess said as she and Allie headed toward the mess hall.

"Well, that went great!" said Hannah happily. "I just know I'll be friends with those guys." She looked at Adora. "You don't seem very excited."

"Oh, I am," Adora said. She sighed. There was another of those little light lies. But that would be her last on Wishworld. "It's just that now my mission is over and we have to leave."

Hannah's face fell. "You won't even stay for lunch?"

Adora was about to say yes, but Cassie elbowed her. "It's time to go back," Cassie said gently.

"Of course." Adora tried to sound brisk and unemotional, the way she normally would. But her voice broke. "You are a true friend, Hannah," she told her Wisher. "I haven't laughed this hard since I was a wee Starling." Two big tears rolled down her cheeks. *Again!* thought Adora. That was really too much. "I'll always remember you."

"And I'll remember you," said Hannah.

Adora knew that wasn't true; Hannah wouldn't remember a thing. All Adora had to do was hug her Wisher and Hannah's memory (and everyone else's) would be wiped clean. She'd have no idea who Adora was and would certainly not remember anything about Starland. Adora thought it kinder not to tell her.

"I almost forgot!" Hannah said. "I made you something in arts and crafts." She reached into her pocket and drew out a long multicolored braid. "It's a friendship bracelet," she explained.

"I love it!" exclaimed Adora. She held out her wrist and Hannah fastened the bracelet.

"It's time to go," Cassie reminded her.

Half smiling, half frowning, Adora hugged Hannah. When she moved away, Hannah looked at her blankly.

"Are you new at Moose Lake?" she asked.

Adora shook her head. "No, we're just visiting to see if we'd like to work here next summer." *Oops!* That was definitely the last little light lie.

"Oh, you would love it here!" Hannah said, smiling. "Everyone is so friendly!"

Who knew? Maybe Adora hadn't lied. Maybe somehow she'd find her way back. She could be one of Hannah's summer friends who came back year after year.

Adora wanted to believe it so badly she almost did.

"Good-bye, Hannah," she said as she and Cassie walked away.

"Wait!" called Hannah. "How do you know my name?"

It took all her strength, but Adora didn't turn around. She just looked ahead toward the clearing, where she and Cassie would unfold their shooting stars and take off for home.

Epilogue

Adora was sitting between Cassie and Tessa in Lady Stella's office. Somehow, she'd wound up by the two Star Darlings with whom she'd shared missions. Fitting for the Wish Orb ceremony, she supposed.

Adora noted the mood around the table. Everyone was subdued. They all spoke in hushed tones, even when they congratulated her, as if acting too happy would make the Starland situation worse.

Adora was quiet, too, thinking wistfully of Hannah and Moose Lake Camp. She touched her bracelet. *Why do they even call it Moose Lake?* she wondered. She hadn't seen any actual creatures that looked like the camp logo. Uncle Hal should really change the name to Bee Lake Camp. Or Clover Lake. Or even Poison Ivy Lake.

"Star greetings, Star Darlings," said Lady Cordial, interrupting Adora's thoughts as she glided into the room. Everyone nodded in a tense way, not quite meeting her eyes.

Abruptly, Adora was brought back to Starland. "What happened while we were gone?" she whispered to Tessa.

"Well . . ." Tessa settled in like she was about to tell a long, involved story. "Leona has been acting all strange and quiet. Gemma told me she even canceled band practice. Leona said she needed to think, of all things! Not sing! And there have been a few more blackouts. They're happening more and more often. But really nothing major."

Not too long before, one energy outage would have been news. Now it was almost expected. And the shortage would only get worse. Yes, Adora had had a successful mission. Yes, she'd collected wish energy. But with outages happening so frequently, it was clear it would not be enough.

Lady Stella gazed around the room. "Girls, your colors seem muted. Please know I am here for you. You can talk to me if you wish, anytime, anyplace."

Next to Adora, Cassie stiffened. *She doesn't believe a word Lady Stella is saying,* Adora thought. *But she wants to.*

"Adora," Lady Stella said, "well done, despite the obstacles you faced. Starkudos to you. As you all must realize, though, as important as these energy-collecting missions are, they may not be enough to turn the tide that has begun. But let us not lose hope."

Then Lady Stella brought out Adora's Wish Orb. The glowing ball floated to Adora, then shifted into the loveliest flower Adora had ever seen: the blue sky-winkle, its corona petals blazing like the Wishworld sun and glittering with stardust.

Slowly, a crystal rose from its center. It was a shimmering stone of blue cylinders hanging together like icicles under a golden dome. Just holding it made Adora feel stronger.

There were some halfhearted oohs and ahhs. Quietly, the girls filed out of the office. In silent agreement, they all returned to their rooms.

Adora stretched out on her bed, happy to be back. She eyed the sequins experiment still spread out over the lab table. Maybe she'd get to it later. Maybe she wouldn't. Right then fashion could wait. Energy science would be her focus.

Across the room, Tessa pulled out astromuffins from her micro-zap. Absently, she put them aside, not bothering to take one—or offer Adora one, either. *Everyone is trying to figure out Lady Stella and the energy problems,* Adora thought. And it was taking its toll. Maybe that was why Leona was staying quiet, too.

As if she had summoned the Star Darling with her thoughts, Adora's Star-Zap buzzed with a holo-text from Leona. It was to the Star Darlings group, and Adora read it quickly: *Come to my room right this starmin! I have something to tell you.*

Adora sighed. Why couldn't she have talked to them when they were all together at the ceremony? Leave it to the star-diva to make a big deal out of nothing. *Forget about Leona thinking deep thoughts about wish energy,* Adora thought, annoyed that she'd have to leave her room before she'd really relaxed. Leona probably wanted them to admire a new song or help choose an outfit for a performance.

Reluctantly, she and Tessa made their way to Leona's room. Before they could even knock, Scarlet opened the door, eagerly beckoning them inside.

Now that's surprising, Adora thought. *Since when does Scarlet get excited about anything Leona does?*

The rest of the Star Darlings were already there, gathered around the star-shaped platform as they'd been before Adora's mission. But now Leona stood in the center of the star, no microphone in sight.

She began to talk before Adora could even sit down. "You might have noticed I've been quiet lately," she told the girls. "I have been spending time on my own, thinking."

Adora waited for Scarlet to make a starcastic comment. But the loner Starling, usually so quick to put Leona down, just nodded.

"I found something the other starday," Leona continued, "when we snuck into Lady Stella's office. And I need to share it with all of you. Scarlet and I have already discussed it. And we feel exactly the same way."

"Did you see something in Lady Stella's desk drawer?" Cassie asked. "When you said you were startled by a rainbow orb spider?"

Leona nodded. "Yes. I didn't see a spider. I saw this."

She opened her hand. And there, in her palm, sat her old, blackened Wish Pendant.

The pendant had been a beautiful golden metallic cuff. Leona had worn it proudly on her upper arm, the star at its center glowing brightly. Now it was burnt and ugly.

Scarlet looked directly at Sage and Libby, Lady Stella's two biggest supporters. Then she turned to Adora. "There's your proof. Leona's Wish Pendant, hidden in her desk drawer. Lady Stella is guilty."

"That's right," Leona said, her voice fierce and serious. "She never brought it to the lab or had a wish scientist examine it. She never tried to figure out why it burned or what happened. And she said she would! She lied.

"You know," Leona continued, a note of pride creeping into her voice, "I did grant a double wish. So the pendant could still have had some energy. But now we'll never know."

"Why wouldn't Lady Stella try to fix the Wish Pendant?" asked Scarlet, sounding like Cassie's uncle's fictional detective. She moved to stand next to Leona. Then she actually linked her arm through the other Starling's. "Lady Stella wants the pendant to stay broken. She doesn't want the energy. That would help the energy crisis. And she doesn't want it to help because—"

"She's responsible for it!" Leona finished.

Some girls gasped. Some nodded. No one spoke in Lady Stella's defense.

Slowly, Adora stood up to join Scarlet and Leona. She'd thought and she'd thought; she'd gone over the evidence again and again her last night on Wishworld. And now she'd drawn a conclusion.

This was the final proof she needed. "I'm with you," she told them.

One by one, the other Star Darlings stood up to form a tight circle. Sage, the last to stand, looked grim. The Star Darlings linked arms, frowning, teary, determined.

"We know what we have to do," said Cassie. The girls all nodded.

Adora thought about lies and truths, about right and wrong. In the end, the evidence was clear. There were no fuzzy half-truths. No little light lies. Lady Stella was guilty.

And the Star Darlings had to turn her in.

Glossary

Astromuffin: A delicious baked breakfast treat.

Azurica: Adora's Power Crystal—rectangular blue pillars of various sizes dangling from a golden dome.

Bad Wish Orbs: Orbs that are the result of bad or selfish wishes made on Wishworld. These grow dark and warped and are quickly sent to the Negative Energy Facility.

Big Dipper Dormitory: Where third- and fourth-year students live.

Bitbat: A small winged nocturnal creature.

Bot-Bot: A Starland robot. There are Bot-Bot guards, waiters, deliverers, and guides on Starland.

Bright-burner: A heating apparatus used in chemistry experiments.

Bright Day: The date a Starling is born, celebrated each year like a Wishling birthday.

Celestial Café: Starling Academy's outstanding cafeteria.

Chatterburst: An orange flower that turns to face whoever is near to capture attention.

Cosmic Transporter: The moving sidewalk system that transports students through dorms and across the Starling Academy campus.

Countdown Clock: A timing device on a Starling's Star-Zap. It lets them know how much time is left on a Wish Mission, which coincides with when the Wish Orb will fade.

Crystal Mountains: The most beautiful mountains on Starland. They are located across the lake from Starling Academy.

Cycle of Life: A Starling's life span. When Starlings die, they are said to have "completed their Cycle of Life."

Druderwomp: An edible barrel-like bush capable of pulling up its own roots and rolling like a tumbleweed, then planting itself again.

Florafierce: A red flower with a ring of longer petals that surround a center mound of small, tightly packed leaves.

Flutterfocus: A Starland creature similar to a Wishworld butterfly but with illuminated wings.

Galliope: A sparkly Starland creature similar to a Wishworld horse.

Glion: A gentle Starland creature similar in appearance to a Wishworld lion but with a multicolored glowing mane.

Glitterbees: Blue-and-orange-striped bugs that pollinate Starland flowers and produce a sweet substance called delicata.

Glorange: A glowing orange fruit. Its juice is often enjoyed at breakfast time.

Glowzene: A chemical substance used in chemistry experiments.

Goldenella: A tall slender tree with golden blossoms that pop off the branches.

Good Wish Orbs: Orbs that are the result of positive wishes made on Wishworld. They are planted in Wish-Houses.

Halo Hall: The building where Starling Academy classes are held.

Holo-text: A message received on a Star-Zap and projected into the air. There are also holo-albums, holo-billboards, holo-books, holo-cards, holo-communications, holo-diaries, holo-flyers, holo-letters, holo-papers, holo-pictures, and holo–place cards. Anything that would be made of paper or contain writing or images on Wishworld is a hologram on Starland.

Hydrong: The equivalent of a Wishworld hundred.

Illumination Library: The impressive library at Starling Academy.

Impossible Wish Orbs: Orbs that are the result of wishes made on Wishworld that are beyond the power of Starlings to grant.

Lightentific method: The scientific protocol that Adora follows when conducting experiments.

Lightning Lounge: A place on the Starling Academy campus where students relax and socialize.

Lightyard: A braided or woven length of material, like a Wishworld lanyard.

Little Dipper Dormitory: Where first- and second-year students live.

Lumin: A unit of liquid measurement used in chemistry.

Luminous Lake: A serene and lovely lake next to the Starling Academy campus.

Mirror Mantra: A saying specific to each Star Darling that when recited gives her (and her Wisher) reassurance and strength. When a Starling recites her Mirror Mantra while looking in a mirror, she will see her true appearance reflected.

Moonberries: Sweet berries that grow on Starland. They are both Tessa's and Lady Stella's favorite snack.

Moonium: An amount similar to a Wishworld million.

Ozziefruit: Sweet plum-sized indigo fruit that grows on pink-leaved trees and is usually eaten raw or cooked in pies.

Power Crystal: The powerful stone each Star Darling receives once she has granted her first wish.

Pricklepine: A spine-covered animal similar to a Wishworld porcupine.

Radiant Hills: An exclusive neighborhood in Starland City where Adora's parents own a clothing store.

Radiant Recreation Center: The building at Starling Academy where students take Physical Energy, health, and fitness classes. The rec center has a large gymnasium for exercising, a running track, areas for games, and a sparkling star-pool.

Reliquaday: The first starday of the weekend. The days in order are Sweetday, Shineday, Dododay, Yumday, Lunaday, Bopday, Reliquaday, and Babsday. (Starlandians have a three-day weekend every starweek.)

Shooting stars: Speeding stars that Starlings can latch on to and ride to Wishworld.

Skywinkle: Adora's Wish Blossom—a blue flower that sparkles as if dusted with diamonds.

Sparkle shower: An energy shower Starlings take every day to get clean and refresh their sparkling glow.

Star ball: An intramural sport that shares similarities with soccer on Wishworld, but star ball players use energy manipulation to control the ball.

Starcar: The primary mode of transportation for most Starlings. These ultrasafe vehicles drive themselves on cushions of wish energy.

Star Caves: The caverns underneath Starling Academy where the Star Darlings' secret Wish-Cavern is located.

Starf!: A Starling expression of dismay.

Star flash: News bulletin, often used sarcastically.

Starfuric acid: A potent chemical used in chemistry experiments.

Star Kindness Day: A special Starland holiday that celebrates spreading kindness, compliments, and good cheer.

Starkudos: An expression used to give credit to a Starling for a job well done.

Starland City: The largest city on Starland, also its capital.

Starlings: The glowing beings with sparkly skin who live on Starland.

Star Quad: The center of the Starling Academy campus. The dancing fountain, band shell, and hedge maze are located here.

Star salutations: The Starling way to say "thank you."

Staryear: A time period on Starland, the equivalent of a Wishworld year.

Star-Zap: The ultimate smartphone that Starlings use for all communications. It has myriad features.

Stellation: The point of a star. Halo Hall has five stellations, each housing a different department.

Supernova: A stellar explosion. Also used colloquially, meaning "really angry," as in "She went supernova when she found out the bad news."

Time of Letting Go: One of the four seasons on Starland. It falls between the warmest season and the coldest, similar to fall on Wishworld.

Time of Lumiere: The warmest season on Starland, similar to summer on Wishworld.

Time of New Beginnings: Similar to spring on Wishworld, this is the season that follows the coldest time of year; it's when plants and trees come into bloom.

Time of Shadows: The coldest season of the year on Starland, similar to winter on Wishworld.

Toothlight: A high-tech gadget Starlings use to clean their teeth.

Twinkle-oxide: A compound used in chemistry experiments.

Wish Blossom: The bloom that appears from a Wish Orb after its wish is granted.

Wish energy: The positive energy that is released when a wish is granted. Wish energy powers everything on Starland.

Wisher: The Wishling who has made the wish that is being granted.

Wish-Granters: Starlings whose job is to travel down to Wishworld to help make wishes come true and collect wish energy.

Wish-House: The place where Wish Orbs are planted and cared for until they sparkle. Once the orb's wish is granted, it becomes a Wish Blossom.

Wishlings: The inhabitants of Wishworld.

Wish Mission: The task a Starling undertakes when she travels to Wishworld to help grant a wish.

Wish Orb: The form a wish takes on Wishworld before traveling to Starland. There it will grow and sparkle when it's time to grant the wish.

Wish Pendant: A gadget that absorbs and transports wish energy, helps Starlings locate their Wishers, and changes a Starling's appearance. Each Wish Pendant holds a different special power for its Star Darling.

Wishworld: The planet Starland relies on for wish energy. The beings on Wishworld know it by another name—Earth.

Wishworld Outfit Selector: A program on each Star-Zap that accesses Wishworld fashions for Starlings to wear to blend in on their Wish Missions.

Wishworld Surveillance Deck: A platform located high above the campus, where Starling Academy students go to observe Wishlings through high-powered telescopes.

Zing: A traditional Starling breakfast drink. It can be enjoyed hot or iced.

Acknowledgments

It is impossible to list all of our gratitude, but we will try.

Our most precious gift and greatest teacher, Halo; we love you more than there are stars in the sky . . . punashaku. To the rest of our crazy, awesome, unique tribe—thank you for teaching us to go for our dreams. Integrity. Strength. Love. Foundation. Family. Grateful. Mimi Muldoon—from your star doodling to naming our Star Darlings, your artistry, unconditional love, and inspiration is infinite. Didi Muldoon—your belief and support in us is only matched by your fierce protection and massive-hearted guidance. Gail. Queen G. Your business sense and witchy wisdom are legendary. Frank—you are missed and we know you are watching over us all. Along with Tutu, Nana, and Deda, who are always present, gently guiding us in spirit. To our colorful, totally genius, and bananas siblings—Patrick, Moon, Diva, and Dweezil—there is more creativity and humor in those four names than most people experience in a lifetime. Blessed. To our magical nieces—Mathilda, Zola, Ceylon, and Mia—the Star Darlings adore you and so do we. Our witchy cuzzie fairy godmothers—Ane and Gina. Our fairy fashion godfather, Paris. Our sweet Panay. Teeta and Freddy—we love you all so much. And our four-legged fur babies—Sandwich, Luna, Figgy, and Pinky Star.

The incredible Barry Waldo, our SD partner. Sent to us from above in perfect timing. Your expertise and friendship are beyond words. We love you and Gary to the moon and back. Long live the manifestation room!

Catherine Daly—the stars shined brightly upon us the day we aligned with you. Your talent and inspiration are otherworldly; our appreciation cannot be expressed in words. Many heartfelt hugs for you and the adorable Oonagh.

To our beloved Disney family. Thank you for believing in us. Wendy Lefkon, our master guide and friend through this entire journey. Stephanie Lurie, for being the first to believe in Star Darlings. Suzanne Murphy, who helped every step of the way. Jeanne Mosure, we fell in love with you the first time we met, and Star Darlings wouldn't be what it is without you. Andrew Sugerman, thank you so much for all your support.

Our team . . . Devon (pony pants) and our Monsterfoot crew—so grateful. Richard Scheltinga—our angel and protector. Chris Abramson—thank you! Special appreciation to Richard Thompson, John LaViolette, Swanna, Mario, and Sam.

To our friends old and new—we are so grateful to be on this rad journey that is life with you all. Fay. Jorja. Chandra. Sananda. Sandy. Kathryn. Louise. What wisdom and strength you share. Ruth, Mike, and the rest of our magical Wagon Wheel bunch—how lucky we are. How inspiring you are. We love you.

Last—we have immeasurable gratitude for every person we've met along our journey, for all the good and the bad; it is all a gift. From the bottom of our hearts we thank you for touching our lives.

Shana Muldoon Zappa is a jewelry designer and writer who was born and raised in Los Angeles. She has an endless imagination and a passion to inspire positivity through her many artistic endeavors. She and her husband, Ahmet Zappa, collaborated on Star Darlings especially for their magical little girl and biggest inspiration, Halo Violetta Zappa.

Ahmet Zappa is the *New York Times* best-selling author of *Because I'm Your Dad* and *The Monstrous Memoirs of a Mighty McFearless*. He writes and produces films and television shows and loves pancakes, unicorns, and making funny faces for Halo and Shana.

Sneak Peek
Clover's
Parent Fix

An important announcement! The whole school had to be there! Would the assembly be about Lady Stella and her role in the energy shortage? About her sabotage?

Clover flipped out of her hammock, landing perfectly on two feet with her arms high above her head. The somersault was really just a habit. But still she glanced at Astra to see if her roommate had noticed.

Astra, a star athlete, had recently returned from a Wishworld mission where she'd helped grant the wish of a young gymnast and had gone to a competition. Now Astra was projecting a holo-sign with the score 999,999.5.

"Starf!" said Clover. "Half a point more and I'd have a perfect moonium."

"Better luck next time," Astra said. "And I'm sure there will be a next time."

"And I'm sure you'll be there to judge me," Clover shot back with a grin.

Acrobatic tricks, kidding around—it all came naturally to Clover. Growing up as part of the Flying Molensa family, Clover had been surrounded by generations of aunts, uncles, and cousins—not to mention her own parents and siblings—all of whom could walk a tightrope while juggling a glowzen ozziefruits and cracking jokes. Living with Astra had always been a breeze. But living in a dorm at Starling Academy was another story.

Before school, Clover had never stayed anywhere for more than a starweek. She and her family traveled year-round across Starland, living out of suitcases on the circus swift train.

Clover had shared a sleeping car with her sisters and she'd always had an upper berth. That was why she loved her hammock bed. It reminded her of the gentle motion of the moving swift train.

"So," said Astra, slipping into her sneakers, "I wonder who will be making this big announcement. Surely not Lady Stella."

Wouldn't it be starmazing, though, if Lady Stella called the assembly and everything is back to normal? Clover thought with a sigh. She imagined the school day proceeding just as it always had, with no energy blips, no upheaval, and Lady Stella just where she should be.

"Starland to Clover! Starland to Clover!" Astra snapped her fingers star inches from Clover's face. "Come on. We'd better hurry. If the entire school is going to the Astral Auditorium, it will be crowded."

Clover nodded, picking up her hat and placing it on her head. She tucked her short purple hair into her trademark purple fedora, making sure it curved just right.

The hat had been handed down to her by her great-grandma Sunny, and Clover planned to pass it down to her own grandchild one starday. It set off her sparkly eyes and short bouncy hair, matching their deep purple shade almost perfectly. And she rarely went out without it.

"Ready," she told Astra.

The two Starlings headed outside and jumped onto the already crowded Cosmic Transporter. All around them, girls chatted excitedly, making guesses about the important announcement.

"Hey, Clover!" a third-year student named Aurora called out. "Maybe Lady Stella is canceling classes because your family is performing."

Last staryear, Clover's family had visited, and Lady

Stella had announced a holiday so the students could watch their show. Everyone had agreed the best part was when Professor Dolores Raye was invited into the star-ring.

Professor Dolores Raye was short—in size and temperament—and wore serious large-framed glasses. She was no one's favorite teacher. So when Clover's dad offered her his arm and led her to a cosmic cannon, the students watched with interest. Clearly, the humorless teacher hadn't wanted to become a Starling cannonball. But at that point, there was no turning back. Clover's dad lit the fuse with a wish-energy snap of his fingers, and she'd flown through the air.

"There's no landing pad!" Lady Cordial had screeched in panic.

Everyone had gasped. But Clover's dad slowed the flight with a wave of his arm and Professor Dolores Raye had landed safely on her feet.

It had been fun. But today's announcement had nothing to do with her family, Clover felt sure.

"No, no," she quickly said. "The circus isn't coming!"

"Well, maybe Lady Stella will hand out the Triple S award today," someone else guessed.

The Silver Shining Star was the highest honor in all of Starling Academy, given to a student who received star-perlative assessments in the classroom, in the school community, and in her hometown.

"Maybe," Clover said pleasantly. She'd be starprised if this announcement brought any good news. But she couldn't exactly explain her thoughts to anyone but a Star Darling.

Once they were outside, three Star Darlings came up behind Clover and Astra: first year Libby and sisters Tessa and Gemma. They all looked worried.

"Star greetings," Gemma said in a quiet voice—at least, quiet for Gemma. As the Cosmic Transporter moved along, she kept up a steady stream of chatter, touching on everything but Lady Stella and the announcement. *And who can blame her?* Clover thought, only half listening. They couldn't discuss anything there in public. Only sweet-tempered, pink-haired Libby paid attention to Gemma, nodding at every statement.

"Did you hear that noise?" Gemma said in a much louder voice. "That rumbling sound? Something must be wrong with the transporter! Remember when it ran out of power just the other—"

"Relax, Gemma," Tessa said irritably. "It's only my stomach. You do know breakfast is postponed because of this assembly, don't you? It's really not fair. Some of us need to eat on a regular schedule."

Clover understood the part about keeping a schedule. She liked to have a predictable timetable, too. But how could Tessa be concerned about food at a time like that? "Tessa—" she began to scold.

But then Piper slid into place beside her and put a reassuring hand on her arm. How did Piper do that? Always appearing seemingly out of thin air? "Relax, Clover," she said in a soothing voice. "Tessa isn't really worried about breakfast. It's just transarence—'transference,' as Wishlings would say."

"Transtarence?" Clover repeated. Sometimes Piper had an intuitive sense of others' thoughts and feelings, but sometimes she was way off starbase. Which would it be now?

"Yes. Tessa is transferring, or redirecting, her concern about Lady Stella," Piper finished in a whisper. "To food!"

Ahead, the Cosmic Transporter was emptying, and Clover realized they had reached the auditorium. She linked arms with Astra and Piper and, with Gemma, Tessa, and Libby close behind, followed the crowd.

Just outside the auditorium doors, the rest of the Star Darlings waited.

"Over here!" Leona waved her arms dramatically, her golden curls bouncing. Cassie stood next to her, looking pale. She seemed to be holding on to Sage's arm for support. The roommates had disagreed about Lady Stella, Sage supporting the headmistress, Cassie opposing her. Sage had a strong personality. But shy, quiet Cassie had stood her ground, convincing the Star Darlings that Lady Stella was the enemy.

Now, looking at Cassie's conflicted expression, Clover thought she could be having second thoughts. Scarlet, a short distance away from the others, looked defiantly at anyone who so much as glanced in her direction.

Meanwhile, Adora and Vega, their blue heads of hair almost blending into one, were huddled over one of Vega's puzzle holo-books. "Hey! Aren't there any science questions?" Adora complained. More transtarence, Clover decided.

"Come on!" Sage said impatiently. "Let's go inside."

The Star Darlings stepped into the auditorium. At the very same starmin, a student named Vivica—just about the meanest girl in school, Clover thought—elbowed her way past, her own group of friends trailing behind her.

Vivica stopped abruptly and the girl behind her tripped, crashing into Clover.

"Star apologies!" the girl told Vivica, ignoring Clover. "I should have been paying more attention."

Vivica sniffed. "Be more careful next time, Brenna." Then she turned to Clover. "As for you, I suggest you try harder to keep up with the crowd. Those SDs," she muttered to her friends. "They really are Superbly Dense!"

Clover ignored her. The Cycle of Life was too short to let Vivica get on her nerves. Unfortunately, she wound up sitting directly behind her in the auditorium.

"I'm really wondering about this big announcement," Vivica was saying to Brenna.

"If it is the Triple S award," Brenna said, "you'll be a star-in."

"Me? Getting the Triple S?" said Vivica with loud false modesty. "Why would they ever give it to little old me? Yes, I was the champion light-skater at the Luminous Lake competition. And I earn all Is in my classes. Illumination, Illumination, Illumination. That's all my star report says! And of course, there's the band I put together. We're totally stellar. Still . . . the award?"

The lights brightened, signaling the students to be quiet. Then Lady Cordial shuffled onto center stage. She gazed around nervously, gripping a microphone in one hand. She tucked a loose strand of purple hair behind her ear, and the mic hit her head. A loud screech sounded, reaching the last rows.

Clover, an old hand at performing in front of an audience, squirmed uncomfortably. Lady Cordial was so awkward and shy. Clover's heart went out to her. Clearly, she wished she was light-years away, not standing onstage about to deliver a major announcement.

"Ahem." Lady Cordial cleared her throat. "S-s-s-s-star greetings, s-s-s-s-s-students," she stuttered.

"Do you know she s-s-s-s-s-s-s-stutters?" Vivica said in a stage whisper to Brenna.

Clover groaned to herself. Why did Lady Cordial always choose words that started with the letter *s*?

"I will get right to the point," Lady Cordial continued.

Clover nodded encouragingly at the stage. Not one S-word in that sentence! That was a start.

Lady Cordial dropped the mic and the thud echoed throughout the room.

"S-s-s-s-s-star apologies!" she cried.

Clover glared around the room, daring anyone to laugh.

"I asked you here today," Lady Cordial said, plowing ahead, a bright purple blush flooding her cheeks, "to relay important news."

Clover sat forward expectantly. This definitely had to do with Lady Stella. Did Lady Cordial know what had happened to her?

"Lady S-s-s-s-s-stella has been unexpectedly called away due to a family emergency."

Okay, Clover thought. *Lady Stella is really gone.* And the family emergency must be an excuse. But Lady Cordial looked like she had more to say.

"As director of admissions, I am next in line," she went on. "S-s-s-s-s-so I will be temporarily in charge."

The room erupted with cries of surprise. Only the Star Darlings remained silent, exchanging looks and worried glances.

Lady Cordial called for quiet. She waved her arms frantically, but the noise didn't subside. Finally, Professor Dolores Raye whistled for everyone's attention, and the students settled down.

Lady Cordial nodded, as if she'd called on the teacher to step in. "I hope everyone will be patient with me. This is a huge s-s-s-s-s-step, with a definite learning curve. It may take s-s-s-s-some time for everything to run s-s-s-s-s-smoothly."

Three S-words, Clover thought. Not quite a record. But she knew Lady Cordial's speech would end with a great big embarrassing double-S phrase. She waited a beat, then nodded as Lady Cordial finished with "S-s-s-s-star s-s-s-s-salutations."